# The Whiskey Haulers

## *by*

# Norm Bass

**First Edition**
**Published by Hooked B Publishing, July 2013**

**Edited By**

Bonnie Bass, Kelly Lyons, Joe Brewer

**Acknowledgment**

Special thanks to the real Nicholas Grant who was the inspiration
for creating the fictional character by the same name.

**Preface**

Both real and fictional places are named in this book. However, the
characters and events portrayed in this book are purely fictional.
The story is in no way intended to reflect on any real persons
including the current or past citizens of any actual places. Any
similarities to real events or actual persons are strictly coincidental
and should not in any way be considered factual.

# Table of Contents

# Chapter One

After spending three months in the canyon lands of Utah rounding up wild mustangs, six men drove the herd to the railhead in Grand Junction, Colorado. The residents of Grand Junction had been anticipating the arrival of the herd for several days and when the herd finally arrived, most of the residents spilled into the streets to welcome the wranglers and take in the once in a lifetime sight of over two hundred horses being driven down Main Street. The entire town seemed to take on a festive atmosphere once the herd arrived and the six wranglers were treated like celebrities. The men were a wild lot with colorful backgrounds and after three months of virtual isolation they were ready to do some celebrating which lasted well into the night.

On the following morning wealthy Colorado rancher, Maxwell Jax, who had organized and financed the venture, met the six men at the Grand Mesa Bank. A photographer for the weekly newspaper was also there and after Jax posed for a few photographs with the men, he paid each of the men, shook their hands, and the adventure was over. The isolation, countless hardships, and encounters with renegade Indians and shootouts with men set on stealing the herd had bonded the men into a tightly knit group over the months, but after receiving their pay and exchanging a few parting words, most of the men shook hands and parted company.

Among the men were two displaced cowboys from Texas named Clyde Decker and Rusty Gibb. The two men had been best of friends since their families settled along the Pecos River in 1854. Together they had fought Comanche, Kiowa, Mexican bandits, and survived the Civil War. But, after twenty years of drifting from one adventure to the next, they were both anxious to return to their family ranches along the Pecos and settle down. So after selling off their personal horses and saddles, they bought some badly needed new clothes and two small canvas roll bags to pack their new wardrobes in and then they walked to the Rio Grande train depot.

"What can I do for you fellas," the railroad ticket agent asked as Rusty and Clyde walked to the ticket window.

"How close can you get us to Texas?" Rusty asked.

"Texas," the man repeated with a surprised look.

"Yeah, that's right," Rusty replied.

"You fellas have got a long train ride ahead of you if you're headin' all the way to Texas."

"Mister, it took us the better part of twenty years to make it all the way out here on horseback. So, I reckon we can handle a few days on a train," Rusty laughed.

"Well, the closest I can get you to Texas on the Rio Grande is to Santa Fe. Once you get there you'll have to buy tickets on the Santa Fe Railroad to take you across New Mexico and on into Texas."

"Okay we'll take two tickets," Rusty said with a happy grin.

"That'll be twenty six dollars apiece," the ticket agent said as he pulled out two tickets and stamped them with the destination."

"What time does the train leave," Clyde asked as he counted out the money for his ticket.

"Well, you already missed the train that would take you through to Durango. But, there's a train bound for Gunnison in an hour. You can take it to Montrose and then catch the southbound from there that'll take you to Ridgeway. You'll have to spend the night in Ridgeway and catch another train tomorrow morning that'll take you on to Durango. Once you get to Durango you'll have to change trains again and that train will take you all the way to Santa Fe."

"You reckon you could write all that down for us?" Clyde asked.

"Sure thing," the ticket agent chuckled.

The last rays of sunlight had already faded and the crescent moon was just rising above the mountains east of Ridgeway when the train pulled into the station. Rusty and Clyde walked the short distance to the hotel where they got a room with two beds and after dropping off their bags and Winchesters, they walked to a nearby café. It was the first time either of them had eaten elk steak and although they both found the steaks quite tasty, they remained partial to a good cut of beef. As they were leaving the café, the sound of honky-tonk piano music lured them into a saloon that was just a little further up the street. Their intent was to have one quick drink, but one led to another and then a red headed saloon gal named, Sally, talked Clyde into a trip upstairs. It was still relatively early when Clyde and Sally concluded their business and if the smile on Clyde's face was any indication, he was a very satisfied customer.

Once they finished off the bottle of rye whiskey that Rusty had purchased to pass the time while he was waiting for Clyde, the two of them left the saloon. They were on their way back to the hotel when two men suddenly appeared out of a dark alley and stuck pistols in their backs. Under normal circumstances, Rusty and Clyde would never have

2

given in to the demands of the two men, but at the time neither of them was in any condition for heroics.

After lifting Clyde and Rusty's Colt revolvers from their holsters, the two men prodded them down the alley at gunpoint. When they reached the end of the alley, the two men ordered Clyde and Rusty to sit on the ground and remove their boots which unfortunately is where both Clyde and Rusty had stashed most of their money. After dumping the cartridges from Rusty and Clyde's pistols, the two robbers tossed the guns aside and picked up the boots.

"If you fellas know what's good for you...you'll stay put until we're out of sight," one of the two robbers threatened.

Once the two men disappeared in the alley, Rusty and Clyde felt around on the ground until they found their pistols. Then they quickly reloaded them with cartridges from their gun belts before going after the men. By the time they reached the street, there was no sign of anyone.

"Son of a bitch!" Rusty said in an angry voice. "Three months of hard work for nothing!"

"At least they left us our boots," Clyde said pointing at what appeared to be two pairs of boots lying in the middle of the street.

Rusty and Clyde retrieved their boots and sat on the edge of the boardwalk to pull them on.

"What are we gonna do now, Rusty?" Clyde asked in a depressed tone.

"Hell, if I know," Rusty replied. "How much money you got?"

"Just a couple of silver dollars," Clyde replied after checking his pockets."

"I got six, myself," Rusty said after checking his own pockets.

"How much you reckon we'll need for those train tickets once we get to Santa Fe?"

"I don't know, but I imagine it'll be more than eight dollars," Rusty replied still angry.

"I guess we're lucky those two robbers left us with anything," Clyde said.

"Yeah, but I smell a rat!" Rusty said.

"Probably some in that alley," Clyde replied.

"I ain't talkin' about that kinda rat, you jug head!" Rusty said becoming angrier. "I'm talking about the two legged kind. Don't it seem awful strange that those men knew we had all our money in our boots?"

"Yeah, now that you mention it," Clyde replied.

"Did you take your boots off when you was upstairs with that whore?"

3

"Well, of course I did. How else could I get undressed and get in bed with her?" Clyde asked with a frustrated look. "You ain't suggestin' she had anything to do with us gettin' robbed... are you?"

"How else would those two men know where we had our money hid?" Rusty asked.

"Maybe, it was just a lucky guess. After all...you wasn't even upstairs. So, how did they know where you had your money stashed?"

"I don't know, but I say we go back in that saloon and have a talk with her!"

"Okay, but don't go accusing her right off. She was a real nice lady."

"They's all nice when you're paying 'em for their services!"

When Rusty and Clyde walked back into the saloon, they paused at the door to have a look around. The piano player was at the bar talking with the bartender and three men that appeared to be locals. Two men sitting at a corner table playing cards looked up briefly and then turned their attention back to their cards as Clyde and Rusty continued toward the bar.

"Where's the red head?" Rusty asked the bartender.

"She's upstairs with a customer," the bartender replied casually.

"How long will she be up there," Rusty asked in an impatient voice.

"Beats me, mister!" the bartender laughed. "Have a drink. I'm sure she'll be down shortly."

"Never mind. Is there some kinda lawman in this town?" Rusty asked.

"Yeah, we got a town marshal. The jail is right up the street."

Rusty turned and walked away without saying anything further and Clyde followed.

"Are you the town marshal?" Rusty asked in an angry tone as he walked into the marshal's office.

"No, the marshal has already gone home, but I'm the deputy," the deputy replied in a casual tone.

"Well Deputy, we just been robbed!" Rusty said still showing his anger.

"Where did it happen?" the deputy asked in a more interested tone.

"In the alley next to the saloon!"

"And let me guess...you had your money stashed in your boots. Am I right?" the deputy asked trying not to look amused.

"That's right," Rusty replied after giving Clyde a surprised look. "How'd you know?"

"Forgive me fellas...but if I had a nickel for every one of you boys from Texas that come in here to make a report after his money was stolen

4

out of his boots, I'd be a rich man," the deputy laughed. "Never could understand why you fellows from Texas always carry your money in your boots."

"We figured that gal my partner hooked up with in the saloon was probably in on it," Rusty said. "She must have told the men that robbed us where we had our money stashed."

"I doubt it, but I'll talk to her," the deputy said, grinning. "Was it Sally, Cindy, Susie, or Roberta that you was with?"

"I can't remember her name," Clyde replied.

"Must have been love at first sight," the deputy chuckled. "What color was her hair?"

"She had red hair," both Clyde and Rusty replied in unison.

"That would be Sally," the deputy said smiling. "Alright, how much did you lose?"

"Nearly three hundred dollars apiece!" Clyde said.

"It's none of my business, but where did you fellas get that kinda money?" the deputy asked with wide eyed expression.

"It was our share of the payoff for a herd of mustangs we spent the last three months rounding up over in Utah," Rusty replied.

"That's a pretty good take for three month's work," the deputy said still looking surprised.

"Maybe so, but it wasn't easy money. We earned every cent!" Rusty said.

"Alright, tell me what happened."

"We was on our way back to the hotel, when two men snuck up behind us, stuck a couple of pistols in our backs, and then they made us walk down that alley next to the Galloping Goose Saloon. Once we were behind the saloon, they made us sit down on the ground and pull our boots off. Then they grabbed our boots and run off."

"I see you both got boots on now," deputy said glancing at their feet.

"Yeah, we found them lying in the street," Rusty replied.

"You got any suspect descriptions?"

"Not really. Like I said, they snuck up behind us."

"Alright, I've made some notes. All I need is your names and where I can get a hold of you in case something comes up."

"I'm Rusty Gibb and this is Clyde Decker," Rusty said with an irritated expression. "We're staying at the hotel, but we was gonna catch the train in the morning."

"We're on our way back to Texas," Clyde added.

"Well, when you get to where you're going, if you want to send me a letter with your addresses, I'll add it to my report before I file it away."

"That's it ...there's nothing else you can do?" Clyde asked.

"Afraid not, fellows."

"But, those bastards took nearly every cent we had," Rusty said. "Hell, we ain't even got enough left over to get us back to Texas and to make things worse...we sold our horses when we was in Grand Junction!"

"I'm sorry, fellas. I don't blame you for being mad," the deputy said in a seemingly sincere and sympathetic voice. "But, I got nothing to go on. I'll sure keep my eyes and ears open for anybody seen flashing a lot of cash around town. But don't forget this is a railroad town and we get misfits and losers through here every day. My guess is those men were probably just a couple of drifters and they probably left town right after they got your money."

"Yeah, I suppose your right," Rusty said in a depressed tone.

"Well, if you need a place to sleep tonight, you can spend the night in one of the cells," the deputy offered.

"No thanks. Luckily, we already paid for our hotel room," Rusty said.

"Don't suppose you know of any outfits doing any hiring this time of the year?" Clyde asked.

"Bad time of the year to be looking for work I'm afraid. Most of the ranches around here got plenty of full time help. About the only time they take on extra hands is in the spring."

"Yeah, I figured as much. I imagine we'll find the same thing in Santa Fe."

"You could probably find work with one of the mines if you want to head on over to Telluride."

"Burrowing in the ground like a couple of critters ain't exactly our kinda work," Rusty replied.

"Well now, I do know of a freight hauling' job," the deputy said with a hesitant look. "If you know how to drive a team and you're pretty handy with those shootin' irons you fellas are packing...you might be interested."

"Is the pay worthwhile?"

"From what I hear... the pay is pretty good...that is if you live to collect it," the deputy said with a straight face. "Last four fellas that took the job ended up dead."

"What were they haulin'... gold?" Rusty asked with a curious look.

"No, but I guess you could say their cargo was worth its weight in gold. They were hauling' whiskey."

"Whiskey?" Rusty repeated with a surprised look.

6

"That's right," the deputy said with another emotionless expression. "Over the years most of the regular freight haulers have been held up once or twice, but for those hauling whiskey, the odds of being robbed goes up tenfold. The whiskey haulers have had entire loads hijacked...wagons and all. Like I said, the last four men that tried taking a load of whiskey from Ridgeway to Telluride ended up dead."

"Why don't all the freight haulers get together and form wagon trains for protection?"

"Worked for the pioneers back in the old days to protect against Injun attacks," Clyde added.

"There's a few that have tried it and some of the freight companies have hired guards, too," the deputy explained. "But, the road over Dallas Divide and on up toward Lizard Head Pass is full of ambush sights and there's lots of places that the road ain't even wide enough to turn a wagon around. The outlaws just sit up in the rocks and pick the drivers and guards off like sitting ducks."

"What about you and the marshal? You're the law. Ain't there anything you can do about it?"

"Well, Mister Gibb, I'm just a deputy town marshal. Me and the marshal got no real jurisdiction outside the town limits and besides that, we got our hands full right here in Ridgeway. The county sheriff is the one that has jurisdiction and he's tried his best to put an end to the holdups. I hear he's even tried to hire a few more deputies, but nobody wants the job because it's too dangerous. Even putting together a posse has become almost impossible for him."

"Well, we gotta do something to raise enough money to get home," Rusty said rubbing his chin. "So, who do we see about getting that whiskey haulin' job?"

"His name is Nicholas Grant. He's the biggest whiskey peddler south of Grand Junction."

"Where can we find him?"

"He's got an office and warehouse over by the railroad yard."

"Okay Deputy, thanks," Rusty said as he turned to leave.

"By the way...if you don't mind... tell Nick I was the one that told you fellows to see him. Never hurts to have a whiskey peddler owe you a favor," the deputy said smiling.

"Be glad to," Rusty said grinning. "What's your name?"

"It's Mike Fish."

"Okay Mike, I'll tell him."

"Thanks, you fellas take care, now."

The following morning Rusty and Clyde stopped by the café for some coffee and then they walked to the rail yard looking for Nicholas Grant's warehouse. The large sign painted on the side of the brick warehouse made the establishment easy to find.

"Nicholas Grant Wholesale Distributor of Fine Spirits," Rusty read aloud. "That must be the place."

"Looks like a big jail. Even got bars on the windows," Clyde commented as he and Rusty walked the short distance to the building.

"Well, if whiskey is as valuable in these parts as that deputy says it is, I imagine it pays to keep it locked up like money in a bank."

Clyde and Rusty entered the door with an "office" sign above it. When they stepped inside it was as if they had just stepped into a six by six jail cell and they were immediately confronted by a man wearing a guard badge and holding a sawed off, double barreled, shotgun.

"Morning gentlemen, what can I do for you?" the guard asked.

"We was hoping to talk to Mister Grant," Rusty replied looking through the bars which prevented anyone from getting beyond the small entryway.

"Is Mister Grant expecting you?"

"No, Deputy Fish told us he might be looking to hire a couple of men to haul whiskey for him," Rusty replied.

"You men must be new around here," the guard said, chuckling.

"You mean because of the way we talk?" Clyde said in a slightly defensive voice.

"Well, I gather from your accents that you men are from Texas, but that's not what I was referring to," the guard said. Then in a very quiet voice he added, "The only men that ever apply for the driver jobs are strangers that don't know what they're getting into. So, if you want some friendly advice...turn around and look for work elsewhere."

"Thanks, but we already heard a little about what we're up against if that's what you mean," Rusty replied. "Unfortunately, we're both flat busted. So, we could really use the money."

"We was robbed last night," Clyde added.

"Yeah, I figured you must have run into some kinda trouble when you mentioned that Deputy Fish was the one that sent you here," the guard said in a friendly voice. "Alright, let me talk to Mister Grant and I'll be right back with you."

The guard returned a moment later and after making Clyde and Rusty hand over their pistols which he locked in a metal box; the guard unlocked the iron jail-like door and led them down a small hallway.

"Here they are, Mister Grant," the guard said as he showed Clyde and Rusty into a well-furnished office.

"Come in fellas, come in!" Grant said in a deep jovial voice with a thick Scottish accent and a friendly smile.

Grant was a large framed, barrel chested man who stood just over six feet tall with a ruddy complexion and a shaved head. He was dressed in gray tweed trousers with a matching vest that appeared to be a size too small.

"So, you're both in need of a job are you?"

"That's right Mister Grant," Rusty replied.

"Call me Nicholas," he said as he extended his massive hand.

"Good to meet you, Nicholas," Rusty said as he shook hands, trying to match Nicholas's grip. "I'm Rusty Gibb and this is my partner, Clyde Decker.

"Aye, nice to meet you fellas," Nicholas replied as he shook Clyde's hand.

"Sit down lads, make yourselves comfortable," Grant said as he returned to the chair behind his large oak desk. "I understand that Deputy Fish sent you fellas to talk to me."

"Yeah, that's right. We was robbed of all our money last night and while we was reporting it to the deputy, he told us you was looking for a couple of men to haul whiskey over to Telluride."

"Aye, and what else did he tell you?"

"He said it was a purty dangerous job," Rusty said with a straight face.

"He said the last four men that took the job ended up dead," Clyde added showing no emotion.

"Aye, then you have an idea of what you might be up against," Nicholas said with a serious look.

"We've had some tough jobs in the past," Rusty said with a confident grin.

"Aye, you look like a couple of men that know how to take care of yourselves," Nicholas said smiling. "But can you handle a team of four mules over rough mountain roads?"

"We've both handled teams before," Rusty replied. "We both drove coaches for the Butterfield Stage Company a few years back. The stage company didn't use mules to pull the coaches, but I imagine a team of overgrown donkeys ain't much different than horses."

9

"No, I suppose not," Nicholas laughed. "Well then, I imagine you fellas can handle the job alright."

"I hate to seem forward, Nicholas," Rusty said still maintaining a straight face. "But, I'd like to know what the job pays before we take it."

"Aye, that's fair enough," Nicholas said with a hearty smile. "Each wagon will be loaded with twenty casks of whiskey and fifty boxes of bottled whiskey. I'll pay you each ten dollars for every full cask of whiskey you get to Telluride and I'll pay you a dollar for every case of bottled whiskey you get there undamaged."

"Just exactly how much does that add up to?" Clyde asked after trying and failing to figure it out on his own.

"That comes to a tidy sum of five hundred dollars," Nicholas replied. "Which is two hundred and fifty dollars for each of you. Providing...you get the entire lot to Telluride in one piece."

"Two fifty...a piece!" Clyde repeated with a broad smile.

"That sounds fair enough," Rusty said. "What about guards?"

"There will be one guard riding along on each wagon."

"Do the guards get the same pay?"

"Aye."

"Well, seeing as how Clyde and I are partners...could one of us be the driver and the other be the guard on the same wagon?"

"I'm afraid not, Rusty. You see I already hired two men as guards. They're both quite skilled with weapons, but unfortunately neither of them can handle a team."

"Mind if I ask how you know they can both shoot?" Rusty asked. "I'd kinda like to know a little bit more about the men that are gonna be responsible for watchin' our backsides."

"Not at all, Rusty. One of the men was a constable for a number of years. The other man is an old friend of mine. He was with William Cody's Wild West Show for a while. Perhaps you've heard of him. His name is Cole Braxton."

"No, can't say I ever heard of him," Rusty said. "But then, I never had any reason to pay good money to watch men pretend they was cowboys fightin' Injuns."

"Hell, we both got plenty of experience doin' the real thing!" Clyde said laughing.

"Well, be that as it may, I've seen Cole Braxton shoot and I assure you he's a crack shot with a Winchester and better than most with a pistol."

"Yeah well, me and Clyde are pretty handy with both ourselves."

"All the better," Nicholas replied. "So, what about it lads...do you still want the jobs?"

"Yeah, I reckon so, Nicholas," Rusty said nodding his head.

"Splendid! I'd say that calls for a drink," Nicholas said as he pulled a bottle and three glasses from his bottom desk drawer.

"It's a little early for me," Rusty said as he glanced at the clock on the wall behind Nicholas.

"Nonsense," Nicholas replied as he poured more than the traditional two fingers of whiskey into each of the glasses. Then after handing Rusty and Clyde a glass, Nicholas raised his glass and said, "To a safe and successful journey!"

"That's purty good whiskey!" Clyde said with a big grin after emptying his glass.

"Aye, have another," Nicholas replied with a satisfied smile after refilling his own glass and then refilling Clyde's. "This is genuine Scotch Whiskey. Not that sheep piss the Irish call whiskey."

"Will we be haulin' some of this here Scotch Whiskey?" Clyde asked with wide eyes and a big smile.

"Aye, but don't be drinking none of that lot in the wagons," Nicholas said shaking a finger at Clyde. "Every bottle you get to Telluride is worth ten times what it's worth here in Ridgeway. You get that load to Telluride and when you come back, I'll give you more than enough whiskey to fill your snoot."

"Don't you worry, Nicholas, when a man trusts us to get a job done, he ain't got nothin' to worry about," Rusty said.

"That's the truth, too, Nicholas. If you was to trust us with a wagon full of virgins...even if they was naked as jay birds...they'd still be virgins when we got to wherever we was goin'," Clyde said with a sincere look.

"Aye... the trick would be finding enough virgins out here to fill a wagon," Nicholas laughed.

"When was you plannin' on having us leave?" Rusty asked.

"I was hoping you could leave early tomorrow morning. No one would expect me to send out a shipment on a Sunday."

"Suits us," Rusty said after glancing at Clyde. "What time tomorrow?"

"I was thinking sometime before sunup would be best. Say around four o'clock," Nicholas replied with a testing gaze.

"Four o'clock?" Rusty repeated with a wide eyed expression.

"Aye, Cole Braxton will arrive by train this afternoon and the gentleman that will be the other guard is already in town. So, I was

11

thinking it would be a good idea to leave while the town was still asleep. I'll have my men bring the wagons inside the warehouse this afternoon to load them and we'll leave them inside tonight. Then we'll hitch up the teams in the morning and the wagons will be ready to go when you fellas get here. That way you'll make it to Placerville before sundown. You can spend the night there and then continue to Telluride on the following day."

"It'll still be dark at four o'clock in the morning," Rusty said in a concerned tone. "Ain't it kinda risky driving wagons through the mountains in the dark?"

"The road between here and Placerville is a fairly good one this time of the year. The roughest and trickiest part of the road is between Placerville and Telluride," Nicholas explained.

"Ain't that also the stretch where all the ambushes have occurred?" Rusty asked.

"Aye...you lads will still need to keep your guard up tomorrow," Nicholas said, taking a boxing stance. "But if them bastards are going to hit you below the belt...it will probably be after you pass Placerville!"

"You talk like you've taken a few punches in your time," Clyde said grinning.

"Aye, that's me in that photograph," Nicholas said with a proud look as he pointed to a photograph on his desk.

"You were a prize fighter?" Rusty asked, smiling as he looked at the photograph.

"Aye, back in me younger days, I was known as Nicholas the Knockout King. Me fans said I had a left as fast as lightening," Nicholas said as he threw a few mock punches.

"No offense, Nicholas...but by the looks of that crooked nose of yours...there must have been a few fellas that was faster," Clyde said chuckling.

"Aye, but it's winning matches that counts not how many times your nose gets broken," Nicholas said with a big grin.

Clyde and Rusty left Nicholas's office a few minutes later and once they were gone, Nicholas wrote a note to Todd Hanley, letting him know that he had hired two drivers and that he planned to send out a shipment the following morning. After sealing the note in an envelope, he had one of his men deliver it to Hanley at the hotel.

***

At about the same time that Rusty and Clyde were meeting with Nicholas Grant, Drew Williams and his partner Bart Taylor were finishing off a pot of black coffee in a rundown, one room, cabin on the other side of town. Drew Williams was a career con artist and thief who could change alliances at the drop of a hat. He had recently fled California after killing his previous partner to hide his involvement in a series of robberies. His current partner, Bart Taylor, was a man of similar character, but with less intelligence and virtually no morals, who had literally killed men for no reason other than the change in their pockets.

"I guess I better take the boss his cut of the money we took off of those two Texans," Drew Williams said after finishing the calculations he was doing on a scrap of brown paper.

"Yeah, I imagine he's already wondering about it," Bart Taylor replied. "You want me to tag along?"

"No, the boss says we spend too much time together as it is and folks around town are starting to notice us," Williams said as he stood up and walked to the door.

When he reached Ridgeway's business district, Williams spotted Jonas Bradley who was the man that recruited Drew Williams and Bart Taylor to carry out the recent string of robberies, hijackings, and murders. Williams quickened his pace and caught up to Bradley as he was crossing the street to his office.

"Morning Boss," Williams said loudly.

"I was just getting ready to come find you," Bradley said after turning around to face Williams.

"Yeah, I figured you were probably wondering about your cut from last night," Drew Williams replied.

"Let's get off the street and talk in my office," Bradley said.

Drew Williams followed Bradley the short distance to his office and once they were inside, Bradley asked, "Were those two suckers from Texas our only pigeons for the night?"

"Yeah, it was awful slow for a Friday night," Williams replied. "We thought Sally had another sucker lined up for us, but as it turned out he barely had enough to pay her for a poke. We could do a lot better if you would let us start rolling some of the locals."

"No, I don't want to stir things up. As long as it's just strangers that are being robbed, folks around town won't get too upset. You start robbing the good citizens of Ridgeway and they'll start putting pressure on the mayor and town council...and the last thing I need is to have them breathing down my neck."

13

"Well, it still wasn't too bad a night," Williams said. "Those two Texans had nearly four hundred dollars on 'em."

"Four hundred! Rita, over at the café, just told me it was more like six hundred."

"Where did Rita hear that?" Williams asked with a surprised look.

"From those two Texans. She said they stopped by the café earlier for coffee."

"You know how Texans love to brag, Boss. They were probably just stretching the truth or trying to impress Rita in order to get into her knickers," Williams said, chuckling.

"Yeah, maybe."

"You know I would never try to cheat you, Boss. Where would the likes of two drifters from Texas get six hundred dollars, anyway... unless they stole it from somebody else?" Williams laughed.

"They told Rita they made it rounding up wild mustangs over in Utah," Bradley replied still somewhat suspicious.

"I swear Boss, all me and Bart got was exactly three hundred and eighty dollars," Williams lied with a crooked smile. "We already gave Sally her ten percent which leaves three hundred fifty two dollars. It's all right here if you want to count it."

"Alright just give me my cut. We got bigger fish to fry, anyway!"

"Any word on when Grant plans on sending out another shipment?" Williams asked as he counted out one hundred fourteen dollars and put it on the desk. "I'm getting awful tired of robbing strangers for pocket change!"

"No, but Rita told me those two Texans were on their way over to see Grant about hiring on as drivers."

"Wouldn't that be great," Williams said smiling. "I'm ready to start making some more big money. What about Hanley? Did Grant hire him as a guard?"

The two men became silent and turned their attention to the door as it opened.

"We were just talking about you," Bradley said to Todd Hanley as he stepped inside the office. "Did Grant buy your story about being an ex-lawman?"

"Yep, he swallowed it hook, line, and sinker," Todd Hanley said with a sly grin. "And I just got a note from him. He's planning on sending out a shipment tomorrow morning before sunrise."

"Before sunrise," Drew Williams, repeated laughing. "What does that old fox think that will accomplish?"

14

"I guess he figures if the whiskey shipment gets out of town with no one knowing, he'll have a better chance of getting it to Telluride," Todd Hanley replied.

"Maybe, we should take the shipment before it gets to Placerville," Drew Williams suggested.

"No, I don't want anything happening that close to Ridgeway," Bradley said quickly. "The last thing we need is the county sheriff poking around in this part of the county. Besides, there's too much traffic on the road between Ridgeway and Placerville. And it would take you nearly twice as long to reach the Ophir hideout which would give the county sheriff too much time to react. No, we'll just pull off this hijacking the same way as we have in the past."

"Okay Jonas, you're the boss," Drew Williams agreed quickly.

"If the shipment is going out in the morning, you and Bart better ride out and round up the rest of the men," Bradley said to Williams.

"Why don't we meet up in Placerville to finalize our plans," Todd Hanley suggested.

"Okay, Bart and I will meet you at the Placerville Palace," Williams replied.

"And I'll see you both back here after you collect the money for the whiskey," Bradley said as Williams and Hanley started to leave.

# Chapter Two

After accepting the job to haul a load of whiskey to Telluride, Rusty and Clyde returned to the hotel and paid for another night's stay which reduced their cash to a mere five dollars and supper that night whittled it down to two dollars. Early the next morning they left their room and walked the short distance to Grant's warehouse. Although the houses were dark and the town was still asleep, Ridgeway was anything but quiet at that time of the morning. The rushing waters of the Uncompahgre River seemed much louder and more predominant in the cool morning air. A few blocks away, a dog barked at the nearly full moon that was now sitting on the western horizon, casting eerie shadows throughout town. The slow, steady huffing sound from the locomotive resting by the coaling tower in the railroad yard was occasionally interrupted by the loud hiss of steam from the boiler's relief valve.

"Glad we decided to wear our long handles," Clyde said. "It's downright chilly up here in these mountains."

"Yeah, it sure don't seem like July," Rusty agreed.

When Clyde and Rusty entered the warehouse, Nicholas was waiting and the worried look on his face immediately showed his relief.

"Good morning, lads," Nicholas said with a big smile.

"Mornin'," Clyde and Rusty replied in unison.

"I was beginning to think that maybe, you changed your minds," Nicholas said as he unlocked the steel barred door in the entryway.

"No sir, once we take a job we see it through till the end," Rusty replied.

"Are the other fellas already here?" Clyde asked.

"Aye, we're just waiting on you fellas. The wagons are loaded and the mules are all hitched up and ready to go."

Clyde and Rusty followed Nicholas down the hallway past his office and into the warehouse portion which took up most of the building.

As Nicholas introduced the four men to one another, they shook hands, but they were all too busy sizing each other up to exchange many words.

Cole Braxton was a man with rugged features of average height with wide shoulders. He was older than Rusty and Clyde had anticipated, but he appeared to be fit and he had a certain air of confidence about him. Beneath his wide brimmed Stetson was a full head of salt and pepper hair that was neatly trimmed as was his thick mustache. His blue flannel shirt was slightly faded, but it was clean and neatly pressed as were his brown trousers that he wore tucked into his recently polished, black, stove pipe boots. An ivory handled colt was strapped on his hip and he held a fancy model 1876 Winchester with various special order options in his left hand.

Todd Hanley appeared to be in his mid-thirties. He stood just under six feet tall with raven black hair that extended just below his collar and a thin mustache that barely stood out against the two day's stubble that covered the rest of his face. He was dressed in ordinary clothes that had seen plenty of wear, but they were clean and in good condition. He had a standard Colt peacemaker in a cross draw holster on his hip and a model 73 Winchester of the same caliber in his hand.

Because Todd was familiar with the road between Ridgeway and Telluride and because Clyde had slightly more experience handling a team than Rusty, it was decided that Todd and Clyde would take the lead wagon. Both Clyde and Rusty took a few minutes to get acquainted with their teams while looking over the harnesses and then they spent a few minutes inspecting the wagons. Once they were satisfied that everything was to their liking, the men boarded the wagons. A couple of Nicholas's men opened the large double doors at the rear of the warehouse and Clyde started his team.

The faint creaking of the wagons and the jingle of the harness hardware blended in with the other sounds of the morning which seemed to have no effect on the residents of Ridgeway.

"I understand you was a trick shooter in a Wild West Show," Rusty said once they were well out of town. "I never been to one, myself. But, I read about all the goings on in a newspaper once."

"Not just any wild west show...it was Buffalo Bill's Wild West Show!" Cole replied in a proud voice.

"I figured they was all pretty much the same."

"Well, take it from me, Rusty...there's a significant difference! The shows put on by Doctor Carver or those other fellows calling themselves Pawnee Bill and Buckskin Joe...they don't hold a candle to Buffalo Bill's Wild West Show. Hell, I heard there are even a couple of women starting up a Wild West Show."

"How did you go about gettin' hitched up with Buffalo Bill?"

"Well, I wish I could say Buffalo Bill personally sought me out because of my shooting abilities, but to be honest... I just happened to be in the right place at the right time."

"You mean you ain't a crack shot like Nicholas said?" Rusty asked with a slightly alarmed expression.

17

"I imagine I can live up to Nicholas's claims alright, but that's not how I got into Cody's Wild West Show. Bill Cody didn't find out how good a shot I was until after I had already signed on with the show. I just happened to be in Omaha when Cody was putting together his first show back in 1883. He was looking for men that could ride and act like cowboys, and bandits, and such. So, me and a buddy signed on. We got paid a dollar a show to ride around the arena shooting blanks and whooping it up like cowboys. I played just about every part there was in his shows before Cody found out I could really shoot. I even played the part of Indians a few times"

"You don't look like no Injun to me," Rusty laughed.

"Well, after I put on some buckskins, painted my face up with war paint, and put one of those feathered war bonnets...I looked more like an Indian than Sitting Bull himself," Cole chuckled. "Even learned to talk a little Sioux."

"You ever actually do any Injun fightin', Cole?"

"Little bit," Cole said, being more than modest. "How about you?"

"Yeah, Comanche and Kiowa mostly," Rusty replied. Then after a brief silence, he asked, "How long was you with Buffalo Bill's Wild West Show?"

"Two years."

"How come you left?"

"Well, it was a lot of fun at first. Putting on those shows was pretty exciting and the folks that come to watch the shows treat you like you're a genuine hero, or god, or something."

"I imagine there was plenty of gals that come to those shows," Rusty said, grinning.

"More women than you could stir with a stick," Cole said, grinning back.

"Sounds like you was in heaven!" Rusty laughed.

"Yeah, but it gets old after a while. Even after the show is over, you can't really be yourself. You always have to act like the person folks think you are. Besides that, I got tired of moving around all the time. And to be honest...I got tired of tricking people and making them think all those shots were real."

"You mean they ain't," Rusty said with a surprised look.

"Well, some of them are, but those shots where they toss a glass ball into the air and you shoot them with a pistol or a rifle...well the cartridges aren't regular cartridges. They're loaded with birdshot."

"Birdshot!" Rusty repeated with a surprised look. "You mean they're just like small shotgun shells?"

"That's right," Cole laughed. "If we used regular bullets, we'd end up killing folks in the grandstands. And most of those shots that are done from galloping horses...same thing. Only sometimes the cartridges are loaded with crushed walnut shells to keep the crowd from being peppered with lead shot."

"Sounds like all those folks that paid good money to see those shows... got cheated," Rusty said.

"Not at all, Rusty. Those folks didn't get cheated," Cole said after a short chuckle. "Those folks paid their money to be entertained and I assure you every one of them got plenty of entertaining. All you had to do is look at the smiles on their faces as they were leaving to know they got their money's worth. And the people that paid to see Sitting Bull, or Wild Bill Hickok, or Calamity Jane, or any of those other famous people...well, they saw the real thing. And so did the people that came to see live buffalo and all the other animals. Besides that, not everything in the shows is play acting. All the animal tricks, riding tricks, roping tricks, rodeo tricks, and so on...they were all real. People go to wild west shows for the same reason folks go to the circus or a play."

"I never seen any of them either. But, I read about 'em in the newspaper."

"Well, after we get paid, you should set some of that money aside and the first chance you get to see a wild west show, or circus, or a theater play...you should make it a point to go."

"That's a good idea, Cole. I'll do that," Rusty said with a committed look.

Even though Nicholas Grant told all the men that the ambushes had all previously occurred on the other side of Placerville, Cole kept his rifle at the ready and both he and Rusty constantly scanned the road ahead for possible ambush sights.

The sun had already set by the time they reached Placerville, but there was still plenty of daylight remaining. The town of Placerville was a small but thriving town located on the San Miguel River at the intersection of three main roads. The west road went to Norwood, Redvale, Nucla, and a cluster of other ranching and farming communities. The road south went into the heart of the mining district and continued over Lizard Head Pass to Rico and beyond.

Since Ridgeway was the closest railhead to the mining district, the folks of Placerville were accustomed to seeing freight wagons pass through town, but they were also well aware of the rash of robberies and hijackings that had occurred recently. So, the men drew a lot of stares as the wagons rolled through town and the townsfolk speculated on their

19

fates. When the wagons reached the south side of town, Todd instructed Clyde to stop his wagon in front of a large barn.

"Are you, Mister Luze?" Todd asked the man that walked out of the barn.

"Yes, that's right."

"We work for Nicholas Grant," Todd said. "We were told we could put our wagons in your barn for the night and you would see to the mules."

"You bet," Mister Luze replied. "I wasn't expecting you fellas, but I'm glad to see Nicholas is back in business. Anyway, it'll cost you three dollars...But, I'd be happy to take two bottles of whiskey instead."

"The fella in the second wagon will pay you the three dollars," Todd said as he pointed back at Cole.

"Alright then, drive your wagons on in," Mister Luze said as he turned and started walking back to the barn.

Once the wagons were inside the barn, Cole paid Luze the three dollars and then he helped Rusty unhitch the team. As soon as all the mules were out of their harnesses and put in the adjoining corral, the large double doors at both ends of the barn were closed.

"I figure we'd take turns guarding the wagons," Cole said. "Two of us can stay while the other two go get some chow."

"There's no need for two of us to stay. One will be plenty," Todd said with an irritated frown. "There ain't nothing gonna happen while we're in town."

"Well, you're probably right, but Nicholas put me in charge and I'd just feel better if two men stayed," Cole replied.

"You fellas go ahead. Me and Clyde will stay behind," Rusty said quickly.

"Suit yourself," Todd said as he turned and walked toward the doors.

"You fellas sure you don't mind staying. I can stay if one of you wants to go first," Cole said.

"No, go ahead," Rusty replied.

"Alright, I'll be back in a little while."

"That Todd fella seemed a little contrary," Rusty said once he and Clyde were alone.

"Yeah, he ain't a real friendly fella. Ain't much of a talker neither. He hardly said more than a few words during the whole day," Clyde said as he sat down and leaned back against the wagon wheel. "What about Cole? What's he like?"

"He seems like a real likeable fella," Rusty said as he sat down next to Clyde. "Me and him talked quite a bit."

"What did you talk about?"

"Lots of things. I told him about how we rounded up those mustangs over in Utah and he told me about bein' in that Wild West Show. He said there was so many women that come to those shows that you could stir 'em with a stick!" Rusty laughed.

"Hell, if that's the case...maybe, we aughta try to get jobs in one of them Wild West Shows. We can ride and shoot better than most fellas."

"Well according to Cole, a lot of the shootin' and such is just tricks and play acting."

"If it's all tricks and play acting, I wonder why folks go to see those shows."

"Well, lots of folks got no idea what really goes on out west. So, it gives folks a chance to 'sperience it and besides that... they got famous people on display, like Sitting Bull and Bill Hickok. And they got all kinds of animals like long horn steers and buffalo..."

"What kinda a fool would pay money to see a longhorn steer?" Clyde interrupted with a hearty laugh. "Hell, Texas is full of 'em. Folks can see all they want for free!"

"Well, they ain't no more buffalo in Texas. In fact, they ain't hardly no buffalo left anyplace. They's nearly instinct!"

"That ain't right, Rusty," Clyde said with a puzzled look.

"What are you talkin' about?" Rusty asked with an equally confused look. "You know they ain't hardly no buffalo left!"

"Well I know that, but the word ain't instinct!"

"Of course it is...It means there ain't any left."

"No... that ain't the right word!" Clyde insisted.

"How would you know?" Rusty asked with an irritated look. "You spend all your extra time drinking whiskey and chasing whores. Hell, I doubt you can even remember the last time you read anything."

"I can so," Clyde replied in an angry voice.

"I ain't talking about menus or the labels on whiskey bottles, Clyde! I want to know the last time you read a book or a newspaper!"

"I read the pictures just fine," Clyde laughed.

"Looking at the pictures ain't the same as readin'!"

"Alright, I admit it's been a while since I read a book, but there's no sense getting uppity, Rusty. If it weren't for readin' labels on things, couldn't neither one of us read. When we was growin' up, once we was done readin' those primers in first grade, there wasn't nothin' else to read."

"Well, I guess that's the truth," Rusty chuckled. "Remember how mad my Papaw Jack used to get when we would tease him 'cause he couldn't read?"

"Yeah, and I remember how he chased us nearly into the next county with that mesquite switch, too!" Clyde laughed.

"I had no idea he could run that fast."

"Me neither. I couldn't hardly sit on a milkin' stool for a week after he got a holt of us," Clyde said still laughing.

"You remember that story he told us about how the Injuns caught him once when he was huntin' buffalo, stripped him down naked as a jaybird, and then chased him through those cactus beds?"

"Yeah, I remember."

"Well, I never really believed that story until after I saw how fast he was chasin' us that day," Rusty said smiling.

"He sure had some wild stories, alright," Clyde agreed. "Especially, after he'd been pulling on a jug of shine."

"Well, you can't hold a man to everything he says when he's been a drinkin'. Hell, we'd all be a bunch of bald faced liars if that was the case," Rusty chuckled. "Anyway, I imagine at least half of them stories was true."

"Well, he sure was a tough old bird! I'll sure give him that much."

"Toughest man, I ever met!" Rusty agreed with a fond reminiscing smile.

"They ever figure out just exactly how many Injuns he killed before them Comanche stuck all those arrows in him and killed him?"

"No, but I imagine it was a bunch. There was blood sign all around his cabin."

"I don't doubt it."

"Anyhow, I sure loved my Papaw Jack; he was a hell of a man... even if he couldn't read!"

"Yeah well, I still say that word you was talking about ain't the right word," Clyde said.

"Well if you're so smart, what is the right word?" Rusty asked, becoming irritated again.

"I don't know, but it ain't instinct. In fact, I once knew a joke about instinct. I'd tell it to you, but I can't remember exactly how it goes."

Clyde and Rusty continued their good natured bantering until they heard the hinges on the barn door groan at which time they both sprung to their feet and drew their pistols.

"Who's there?" Rusty asked loudly as he held the lantern up.

"It's me, Cole!"

Both Rusty and Clyde holstered their pistols once they saw that it was in fact Cole.

"Don't suppose Todd has been back," Cole said with a slightly annoyed look.

"Not yet," Rusty replied.

"I guess I ruffled his feathers a bit," Cole said. "And he was probably right. There's no reason for two of us to stand guard. So, you fellas might as well go ahead and get yourselves something to eat."

"We ain't really hungry, Cole," Rusty said.

"What do you mean you aren't hungry?" Cole asked with a disbelieving look. "You haven't had anything to eat all day."

"Well the truth is, we're nearly flat broke," Rusty said turning slightly red. "A couple of fellas robbed us night before last."

"We only got two bucks between us," Clyde added.

"So, we figured on saving our money to buy something to eat and maybe get a couple of drinks to celebrate when we got to Telluride,"

"I'll lend you some money," Cole said without hesitation. "You can pay me back after we get paid."

"Well...if you wouldn't mind lending us a couple bucks...we'd sure appreciate it," Rusty said.

"Be happy to. Will five bucks apiece be enough?"

"That'll be plenty," Rusty said with an appreciative smile.

"Alright, here you are," Cole said as he handed both Rusty and Clyde a five dollar gold piece. "I ate at that little café right up the street. The chili was excellent if you want a recommendation."

"Thanks Cole, but I was kinda thinking about seein' what that place up by the crossroads had to offer," Rusty replied.

"The Placerville Palace?" Cole asked smiling.

"Yep. I thought it was kinda of a catchy name."

"By the way Cole, maybe you could settle an argument that me and Rusty was having," Clyde said with a big grin. "What's the word that means they ain't no more? You know like the buffalo...there used to be thousands and now there ain't hardly any."

"You mean extinct?"

"Yeah, that's it...extinct!" Clyde said with a big smile. Then looking at Rusty he said," I told you instinct weren't the right word!"

"Alright, I made a mistake," Rusty admitted blushing slightly. "But, you gotta admit the words sound almost the same."

"Maybe so, but it goes to show you...I ain't as dumb as you think!" Clyde said still grinning. "I remember that joke now, too!"

23

"Come on let's go get something to eat," Rusty said trying to change the subject.

"Don't you want to hear my joke?" Clyde asked wrinkling his brow with an annoyed look.

"Tell me later, after we get something to eat," Rusty replied.

Rusty and Clyde left the barn and walked back to the other end of town which was where the majority of businesses were, including the Placerville Palace. In addition to being the only hotel in town, it also had a bar and adjoining dining hall.

"Hey, there's Todd," Clyde said as he spotted Todd sitting at a table in the bar room with two other men."

"Do those two fellas he's with look familiar?" Rusty asked.

"I don't think so," Clyde said as he gave the men another look.

"They do to me, but I can't remember where I've seen them before," Rusty said, staring at the men.

"Come on let's grab a table in the dining hall before they's all taken," Clyde said as he continued toward the adjoining room which was reserved for diners.

Rusty took one final look at the two men as he again tried to figure out where he had seen the men and then he followed Clyde.

***

The two men at the table with Todd were Drew Williams and Bart Taylor. Because the three men were busy finalizing the plans for the ambush and hijacking of the wagons, none of them noticed Clyde or Rusty when they walked through the bar on their way to the dining hall.

"Wish we would have known there was going to be two wagons," Williams said in an irritated voice. "We were only planning on one."

"Like I said, all Grant's note said was...he hired a driver and I was to be at the warehouse by four o'clock. I didn't know there was gonna be two wagons myself, until I showed up at the warehouse this morning," Todd replied in a defensive voice. "What difference does it make anyway?"

"I just don't like surprises! Besides that if I knew there were going to be three men to deal with, I would have tried to get more men of our own."

"You got four others besides yourselves!" Todd replied. "Six should be plenty! You bring on more men and we'll just have to split the take more ways."

24

"What about that other guard? Do you know anything about him?" Bart asked.

"No, Grant just said he was an old friend," Todd replied.

"That fancy rifle you said he's got makes me nervous," Williams said,

"Just because a man carries a fancy gun, don't mean he knows how to use it," Todd said. "Besides, if you do like I say and make sure your men concentrate on taking him out right from the git go... it won't make any difference if he can shoot or not."

"Be a lot easier if he was on the lead wagon," Williams said continuing to look annoyed.

"I know, but like I said...Grant was the one that told me to ride on the lead wagon," Todd said with an aggravated expression. "But, I'll try to figure out how to get him to switch places with me. Just make sure if I do, you and your men don't start taking shots at me."

"Don't worry, I'll make sure everybody knows that you'll be wearing that same red shirt you got on now," Williams replied.

"Okay, I guess that about covers it," Hanley said as he emptied his glass and stood up. "I better be getting back before Braxton starts to wonder where I am and comes looking for me."

***

Clyde and Rusty ate their supper and after paying the waitress, they walked back into the bar looking for Todd. The bar was much more crowded than it had been when they first arrived. All the tables were occupied and men were lined up elbow to elbow across the bar itself. Once Clyde and Rusty determined that Todd had already left, they made their way to the bar and after treating themselves to a shot of whiskey, they headed back to the barn.

"Pardon me," Rusty said after a belch spontaneously erupted as they were walking.

"That was real nice of Cole to lend us some money," Clyde said.

"Yeah, I told you he seemed like a good man."

"He seems pretty smart, too," Clyde said grinning. "He came up with that word extinct right off the bat."

"You ain't gonna start that again are you?" Rusty asked with an aggravated look. "I already admitted I was wrong."

"No, I was just commenting that Cole seemed like a smart man," Clyde replied still grinning. "Anyhow, you want to hear that joke now?"

"If I say no, you'll just keep on pestering me. So, go ahead," Rusty said in an unenthused tone.

"Okay well, there was this mama skunk...and she had two baby skunks," Clyde said chuckling. "One of the babies was named In and the other was named Out."

Clyde paused to chuckle again and then continued, "Anyway, Out was a good skunk and always stayed real close to his mama, but In was real curious and he was always wandering off and getting lost. So, do you know how the mama skunk found him?"

"Sure...I can hardly wait," Rusty replied in a disinterested voice.

"Instinct," Clyde replied laughing.

"That weren't even funny!" Rusty replied looking annoyed again.

"Don't you get it? Instinct ... In...stinked!"

"I get it, but it ain't funny. In fact...the joke stinked!" Rusty laughed.

# Chapter Three

Once all four men were back at the barn, Cole informed them of his plan to have the men take turns standing guard while the others slept. Todd objected to the idea, saying that he felt it was unnecessary which of course it was, but only he knew that. Regardless, after Cole insisted, the four men drew straws to determine the order in which each man would stand guard. As it turned out, Todd drew the longest straw and elected to take the first watch. Rusty took the second, Clyde the third, and Cole ended up with the last watch from four to six. Clyde and Rusty were quite accustomed to sleeping on the ground and having some straw for extra cushion made it even better. So, while the two of them slept quite comfortably in spite of the constant rustling caused by the large population of rodents in the barn, Todd and Cole spent considerable time tossing and turning or throwing things at the mice.

At exactly six o'clock, Cole woke Clyde and Rusty. Todd was already awake, but still stretched out on his bedroll. After splashing the remnants of sleep from their eyes at the water trough, Clyde and Rusty went to the corral to start bringing in the mules.

"What do you say we switch places today, Cole?" Todd said once Clyde and Rusty were out of the barn. "You ride in the lead wagon with Clyde and I'll ride with Rusty."

"How come?" Cole asked with a curious look.

"I just thought you might be tired of eating dust and I thought it would only be fair to let you ride up front for the day."

"Thanks, Todd that's mighty considerate, but the road wasn't all that dusty."

"Well, to be honest, I was also hoping we could switch places because Clyde starts to wear on you after a while."

"Really?" Cole said with a surprised look. "He seems like a pretty humorous, easy going guy to me."

"Yeah, but you can't get him to shut up!"

"Well, Nicholas was pretty set on you and Clyde taking the lead wagon and me and Rusty following. So, I imagine you can put up with Clyde for a few more hours."

Todd wasn't happy with Cole's response and his expression showed it, but he walked away without voicing further objections.

Once all eight of the mules were harnessed and hitched to the wagons they were each rewarded with a few scoops of grain and shortly thereafter, the wagons were again on their way to Telluride. The morning air was again crisp and a heavy dew covered the ground. The road from Placerville to the small settlement of Sawpit followed the river as it meandered through thick stands of pine and aspen trees, but after Sawpit, the road started to climb out of the valley as it continued toward the 10,000 foot summit of Lizard Head Pass. The sky was clear and the sun intense as the wagons started up the steep grade.

"It's getting damned right hot out here now," Rusty said as he wiped the sweat from his forehead on the back of his shirt sleeve.

"Yeah, it was almost chilly down in valley, but the sun reflecting off these red rocks really warms things up quick," Cole said as he pulled off his plaid wool jacket and reached under the seat for the canteen.

Cole took a long drink from the canteen and then he held the reins while Rusty did the same.

"Hold 'em another minute will you, Cole, while I peel off this shirt," Rusty said as he screwed the lid back on the canteen.

After putting the canteen back under the seat, Rusty removed his shirt revealing the upper half of his one piece red long underwear.

"That's much better!" Rusty said as he placed his shirt under the seat and took the reins.

"When we get up to that bend ahead, let's stop and rest the teams for a few minutes."

"Good idea," Rusty replied.

When Clyde's wagon was just about to the bend, Cole yelled at Clyde and Todd to stop their wagon.

"What the hell does he want us to stop for?" Todd asked in an irritated voice as he turned in the seat to look back at the second wagon.

"Probably wants to rest the team," Clyde replied casually as he pulled the mules to a stop.

Todd's eyes grew wide and a shocked look appeared on his face as he noticed that Rusty had removed his shirt.

"Son of a bitch," Todd cursed under his breath.

Once both wagons were stopped, Rusty set the brake and then he and Todd walked to the lead wagon. "How much further until we get to the Telluride turn off?" Cole asked Todd.

"Couple miles," Todd replied in an uneasy voice.

"Okay," Cole said as he gazed at the road ahead. "I don't like the looks of that open stretch ahead. So after we get going, Rusty and I will hang back a ways and put a little distance between the two wagons."

"What the hell for? Be safer if we keep bunched up," Todd said quickly.

"No, if there are men up in those rocks ahead waiting to bushwhack us, we're better off keeping a little distance between the wagons to make it harder for 'em to concentrate their fire."

"I say we stick together. Doesn't make sense to spread out!" Todd said in a heated tone. "If there are men up ahead and you hang back, how are you gonna help us shoot back?"

"Don't you worry. We won't be that far behind you," Cole said calmly. "We'll be close enough to shoot back, alright."

"I don't like it!" Todd said with an angry look.

"Well, it's not up to you," Cole replied, starting to become aggravated. "Nicholas put me in charge, not you."

"That doesn't give you the right to get us all killed! We all got a stake in this!"

"That's true," Cole said nodding. "Alright... Clyde and Rusty, what about it? Do we stay bunched up or do Rusty and I put a little distance between us?"

"I'm with you, Cole," Rusty said without hesitation. "If there are men up ahead, they'll be able to see both wagons right from the git go once we round that bend. And I doubt a show of force will make any difference and like Cole said...if we hang back a little, they won't be able to concentrate their fire like they could if'n we was bunched up."

"Okay Clyde, what about you?" Cole asked.

"I agree with Rusty. I remember one time when we was worried about being jumped by a bunch of Kiowa and..."

"I've heard enough of your Indian stories!" Todd blurted out interrupting Clyde. Then as he turned and started walking away he said, "Do whatever you want, Cole!"

"He sure is a disagreeable fella, ain't he?" Clyde said with a surprised look.

"I reckon during all those years he was a lawman...he must have got used to having his own way all the time," Rusty said.

"Well, do your best to get along with him, Clyde. We'll be in Telluride in another three or four hours," Cole said looking toward Todd and shaking his head in disbelief.

The men waited until the mules were no longer breathing hard and then they climbed up onto their respective wagons. Once Clyde was on his wagon he too removed his shirt revealing the upper half of his red union suit before starting the team. Rusty waited until Clyde's wagon was about fifty yards ahead and then he slapped the mules on the rump with the reins as he shouted, "Get up there, you overgrown donkeys."

As the wagon lurched forward, Rusty and Cole began to scan the rocks ahead looking for any sign of movement.

"Hey Cole, you said you done some Injun fightin' right?"

"Yeah, a little bit."

"Well, you know that feeling you get when you think a bunch of Injuns is about to jump you?"

"You mean when the hair on the back of your neck starts to tingle?"

"Yep...that's the one," Rusty replied. "I hate to say it, but I got that same feeling right now."

"Yeah, me too," Cole said.

\*\*\*

Drew Williams, Bart Taylor, his brother Mitch, and three other men left their hideout near Ophir before the sun had fully cleared the peaks that made up the eastern horizon. They arrived at their favorite ambush sight about an hour before the two wagons started the climb up the steep grade toward Lizard Head Pass. After hiding their horses into a dense stand of aspen, the men climbed up into a rock outcropping that overlooked a vast stretch of open road and settled in among the rocks.

Two of the men were napping while the others engaged in idle conversation when the two wagons rounded the bend at the far side of the open stretch of road.

"Here they come," Williams said in an excited voice.

"Hey Boss, are you sure Todd said he would be wearing a red shirt? I count three red shirts!" One of the men said almost immediately.

"I know. I see the same thing!" Williams said in an irritated tone.

"You go to be kiddn'!" Taylor said as he got to his feet and peered over the rocks.

"That son of a bitch!" Williams cursed. "Leave it up to Hanley to foul things up."

"If Todd knew some of the others were wearing red shirts...why didn't he pick a different color?" Bart Taylor asked.

"How the hell should I know?" Williams replied in an angry voice.

"What do we do now?" Taylor asked.

"I got a good mind to shoot 'em all down!"

"Even Todd?" Taylor asked with a shocked look.

"It would serve the bastard right!"

"The boss is gonna be awful mad if we go killin' his buddy Todd," Taylor warned with a concerned look.

"How about it, Boss? Who do we shoot at?" one of the other men asked.

"Maybe we should just let 'em pass," Taylor suggested.

"Hell no! I didn't ride all the way out here for nothing!" Williams replied. "Pedro, wait until the first wagon is real close and then shoot one of those mules. At least that'll stop 'em until we figure out who's who."

"If you kill one of those mules, how we gonna get the wagon over the pass? There's no way we can load everything in one wagon," Taylor said with a worried look.

"Three mules should be able to pull the load," Williams replied in an aggravated tone. "If we have to, we can shift some of the whiskey to the other wagon."

"I hope you know what you're doing!" Taylor said still looking worried.

"You got a better idea?" Williams snapped.

Bart Taylor shook his head and looked away to avoid Williams' angry eyes.

"Mitch, Jack, and Brock...you three try to pick off that fellow in the blue shirt on the second wagon. The rest of us will concentrate on the first wagon. But wait until Pedro fires the first shot. Once we get 'em stopped we'll try to talk 'em into giving up."

"What if they won't give up," Mitch asked. "What if they just keep shooting back?"

"Then we'll just have to figure out who the shooters are and pick 'em off one at a time," Williams said glaring at Mitch. "Remember nobody shoots until Pedro kills one of the mules!"

"Hey Pedro," Mitch said loudly. "Let that lead wagon get as close as you can before you shoot, otherwise that second wagon will still be a long ways off."

"Si, I wait until I can see the color of their eyes!" Pedro laughed.

***

The lead wagon was almost directly below the rock outcropping and within a hundred yards of the tree line when a rifle shot broke the relative quiet and echoed across the valley. Clyde struggled to maintain control of his team as the wounded mule brayed loudly while dropping to its knees and the rest of the panicked team fought to free themselves from their harnesses.

Cole immediately jumped off the second wagon and returned fire as Rusty quickly regained control of his own startled team and wrapped the reins around the brake handle. As more shots rang out and a bullet

31

splintered the wood where Cole had been sitting, Rusty grabbed his Winchester and rolled out of the wagon while Cole continued returning fire as rapidly as he could work the lever on his rifle.

"That guy's too good!" Jack yelled as one of Cole's bullets ricocheted off the rocks next to his head causing him to dive to the ground.

"Probably just a lucky shot," Williams yelled back. "Just keep shooting!"

"Yeah well, that lucky shot damn near took my ear off," Jack replied as he wiped bits of rock from his face and then peered back over the rocks.

***

"You okay, Rusty?" Cole asked once the shots from the rock outcropping stopped.

"Yeah, I'm good," Rusty replied from under the wagon.

"Looks like Clyde and Todd are okay, too," Rusty said after glancing at the lead wagon. "But, they got a mule down."

"How about you try to draw their fire and I'll see if I can get a shot?" Rusty said as he racked another round into the chamber of his rifle.

"Okay let me know when you're ready."

Cole removed his hat, flipped up the long range tang sight, and rested the barrel across the top of the wagon side.

"Go ahead, Rusty," Cole said as he took aim at the vicinity of his last shot.

Rusty fired and his shot was answered almost immediately. Cole took careful aim at the spot where the telltale puff of gun smoke appeared from the rocks and squeezed the trigger. His bullet found its mark spraying the surrounding rocks with Jack's blood and brains. Another volley of shots rang out from the rocks and Cole quickly ducked down as several bullets hammered into the opposite side of the wagon.

Rusty returned the fire from under the wagon nearly hitting Mitch.

"Jack was right!" Mitch shouted in a shaken voice. "That one nearly parted my hair!"

"Just keep shooting damn it!" Williams replied in an angry voice. "It was just another lucky shot."

"Maybe, but I'm telling you these guys are awful good," Mitch replied while slowly poking his head over the boulder he was hiding behind.

32

As Mitch again aimed his rifle toward the second wagon, a shot rang out and a bullet split Mitch's head open like an over ripened watermelon spraying Brock with blood.

"Lucky my ass. Let's get out of here!" Brock yelled in a panicked voice.

"Are you okay, Mitch?" Taylor cried out as he looked toward Brock and saw his brother's body slumped down in the rocks.

"He's dead!" Brock shouted back still wiping blood from his face. "And if we don't get out of here...we're all liable to be killed!"

"Alright, let's go," Williams reluctantly agreed. "It's every man for himself. If you make it back to your horse ride out. We'll meet up at the Yellow Canary."

"I can't just leave Mitch," Taylor replied in an angry, almost sobbing voice. "He's my brother!"

"Let's go! There's nothing you can do for Mitch now!" Williams shouted as he began to crawl towards the back of the outcropping.

Cole and Rusty continued to watch the rocks hoping for another shot. They occasionally caught a quick glimpse of the surviving bushwhackers as they crawled on their bellies, making their way to the back of the outcropping, but, they never had a clean shot.

"Looks like they're leaving," Rusty said in a relieved tone.

"Yeah, looks like it," replied Cole. "But we better stay put for a while...just to make sure," then turning his attention to the lead wagon he shouted, "Looks like they're pulling back! But stay low for a while!"

"Clyde's been hit!" Todd shouted back.

"How bad's he hit?" Rusty shouted after scrambling out from under the wagon.

"It looks pretty bad and I need help to stop the bleeding!" Todd replied.

"I better go help him, Cole," Rusty said quickly.

"We'll both go," Cole replied. "I'll cover you and when you get there you cover me!"

Cole again rested his rifle across the top of the wagon and took aim at the rock outcropping.

"I'm ready when you are," Cole said quickly.

Rusty took off running and when he reached the lead wagon without incident, he immediately took up a position near the back of the wagon and motioned for Cole to come ahead. Once Cole also reached the lead wagon without any shots being fired, he and Rusty exchanged quick breathless smiles and then they hurried to the front of the wagon where Todd was kneeling by Clyde.

33

"Drop those rifles and get your hands up!" Todd said as he stood up with his pistol cocked and ready to fire.

Both Rusty and Cole were speechless as they looked at Todd with shocked expressions.

"What the hell are you doing?" Cole asked still looking stunned.

"You heard me...drop those rifles!" Todd ordered.

"You're in with them, aren't you?" Cole asked as he gently laid his Winchester on the ground.

"That's right," Todd smirked.

"Why you no good, double crossing..."

"That's enough!" Todd said loudly, interrupting Rusty. "Just do as I say and drop your rifle."

Rusty bit his lip and looked at Todd with anger filled eyes as he lowered his rifle to the ground and raised his hands.

"Now take off those gun belts and drop 'em," Todd said after Rusty dropped his rifle.

Rusty quickly unbuckled his gun belt, but Cole hesitated and continued to glare at Todd Hanley.

"I'll do anything you say, just let me take care of Clyde," Rusty said as he dropped his gun belt next to his rifle.

"He ain't shot, I just thumped him on the head," Todd said with a sly laugh. Then giving Cole a threatening look, he growled, "I told you to get your gun belt off!"

Cole continued to hesitate, his eyes now full of fire.

"Do it or by god I'll shoot you where you stand!" Todd said in a mean, callous voice.

Cole's eyes remained fixed on Todd's as he unbuckled his gun belt with his left hand while slowly raising his right. As Cole's gun belt started to slip down his side, his right hand dropped with the speed of a rattlesnake strike, grabbing his pistol, and firing it before the empty holster hit the ground. Todd stumbled backwards and fell over as the bullet hit him in the forehead.

Rusty looked at Cole with an astonished look on his face as Cole picked up his gun belt, twirled his pistol, and then stuffed it in the holster.

"I never seen anything like that," Rusty said.

"It was one of the tricks I used to do in Cody's Wild West Show," Cole replied with a blank expression. "I guess all that practice paid off after all."

# Chapter Four

While Rusty tried to revive Clyde, Cole got busy cutting the harness and reins off of the dead mule.

"Welcome back," Rusty said with a relieved smile as Clyde started regaining consciousness.

"What the hell happened?" Clyde asked in a groggy voice as he felt the large goose egg on the back of his head.

"Todd cold cocked you?"

"What the hell did he do that fer?"

"Looks like he was in with those men that bushwhacked us."

"No kiddin'? Where is that son of a bitch?"

"He's dead," Rusty replied. "Cole shot him. Wish you could have seen it, Clyde. Todd had us at gun point. He ordered us to drop our guns and as Cole was letting his gun belt drop he snatched his pistol from the holster and shot Todd dead. It was the most amazing shot I ever saw."

"I told you there was something strange about Todd," Clyde said as he tried to sit up.

"How do you feel?" Cole asked as he joined Rusty and Clyde.

"Like I been kicked in the head by one of them mules," Clyde replied.

"Think you'll be up to sitting on a wagon seat the rest of the way to Telluride?" Cole asked.

"Yeah, this ain't the first time I been knocked out," Clyde said as he tried to stand up.

Clyde's attempt to stand was unsuccessful and he nearly fell over before Rusty grabbed him.

"Don't look like you're in any condition to drive a team," Rusty said as he helped Clyde sit back down.

"I'll be alright, I just need to rest a few minutes," Clyde insisted.

"I don't think so," Rusty said with a short chuckle.

After a brief discussion, it was decided that Rusty would take over the lead wagon and Cole would attempt to drive the second wagon with Clyde riding along as his passenger and driving instructor. So, after helping Clyde to the second wagon, Cole and Rusty stashed Todd's body in the rocks where it could be recovered at a later time. Then after transferring several cases of whiskey to the second wagon in order to lighten the load for the team of three mules, they continued toward Telluride.

They arrived in Telluride a couple hours later without further incident and proceeded down the main street to the opposite side of town where Nicholas Grant's warehouse was located.

"You fellas are a sight for sore eyes!" the warehouse manager said eagerly as the two wagons pulled into the fenced yard adjacent to the warehouse.

"Where do you want us to park these wagons?" Rusty asked loudly.

"Just pull 'em up close to those double doors and my men will start unloading them."

Once the two wagons were by the doors, Rusty set the brake and after wrapping the reins around the brake handle, he jumped down from the driver's seat.

"I'm Charlie Duckfoot. I run things here in Telluride for Nicholas Grant," Charlie said in an excited voice as he extended his hand to Rusty.

"Good to meet you, Charlie. I'm Rusty Gibb."

"I sure am glad to see you, Rusty. Nicholas sent me a telegram that he was sending out another shipment, but to be honest... we weren't sure you would make it."

"Well, as you can see we had a little trouble. Bushwhackers ambushed us just before we got to the turn off. They killed one of the mules, but we managed to run 'em off."

"What happened to the fourth man? They kill him, too?" Charlie asked.

Before Rusty could reply, Cole and Clyde walked up.

"Well I'll be damned," Cole said with a big grin as he recognized Charlie..

"Howdy Cole!" Charlie said with a big smile as he shook Cole's hand. "I nearly fell over when I saw your name on that telegram from Nicholas Grant."

"How have you been, Charlie? What's it been... four years?" Cole asked.

"Been nearly five since I left Wyoming," Charlie replied.

"I guess you're right," Cole said still smiling. "I see you already met Rusty...this is his partner, Clyde Decker."

"Good to meet you Clyde, I'm Charlie Duckfoot," Charlie said, shaking Clyde's hand. "You fellas can't imagine how happy we are to see you. The warehouse is damned near empty and I was beginning to think we never would see another shipment get through. Come next week, I figured me and my three helpers would all be out of a job."

"Well, we're pretty happy about making it, too," Cole laughed. "But, it wasn't just our jobs we were worrying about."

"No, I reckon not," Charlie said with a sheepish smile. "By the way... what happened to the fourth man?"

"Cole shot him!" Rusty said grinning. "Turns out the son of a bitch was working with the bushwhackers. He even cold cocked Clyde and tried to get the drop on Cole and me."

"I'll be damned!" Charlie said with a shocked expression.

"Yeah, and there he was an ex-lawman to boot," Rusty said.

"Well, I still ain't convinced he was actually a lawman," Clyde said. "There was just something about him that didn't seem to add up."

"You probably aughta have a doctor check out the bump on your noggin," Charlie said as he took a closer look at Clyde's head. "There's a doctor's office just a few blocks back up the street."

"That's a good idea," Cole said. "Rusty, why don't you take Clyde to see that doctor while I go report what happened to the sheriff. Then we can meet up later at one of those saloons we passed."

"Sounds good to me," Rusty said. "I could use a drink!"

"Me too!" Clyde said quickly.

"The best saloon in town is the Yellow Canary," Charlie said. "They got the prettiest gals, too."

"Okay the Yellow Canary it is," Cole said. "Charlie, will you watch our stuff for a while?" Cole asked.

"You bet! Everything will be in my office waiting for you when you get back. By the way, when do you fellas plan on taking the wagons back to Ridgeway?"

"If it's all the same to you Cole, me and Clyde would just assume get back to Ridgeway as soon as possible. We're both kinda anxious to continue on to Texas."

"How soon can you get another mule, Charlie?" Rusty asked.

"Probably, by tomorrow morning," Charlie replied. "I'm sure I can trade old man Turner a few bottles of whiskey for one."

"Well then, I guess we'll start back first thing in the morning," Cole replied.

"Okay, me and my men generally get here around seven o'clock," Charlie said. "We'll have the wagons hitched up and ready to go by 7:30."

"Good, we'll see you in the morning, Charlie," Cole replied. Then as he was turning to leave, Cole said to Rusty and Clyde, "I'll see you fellas at the Yellow Canary."

The sheriff's office and county jail was at the far end of town, so it took Cole several minutes to get there.

"Are you the sheriff?" Cole asked the man sitting at the desk when he entered.

"No, the sheriff isn't here right now, I'm Deputy Walters. What can I do for you?"

"I want to report an attempted holdup," Cole replied.

"Okay, what happened?" the deputy asked in a casual voice.

"We were on our way here with two wagon loads of whiskey when we were ambushed."

"Whiskey!" the deputy repeated with a much more interested look. "You're lucky you weren't killed!"

"Well, they tried their best, but we managed to run 'em off?"

"How many were there?"

"Couldn't tell for sure, but I'm guessing there were five or six. Seven... including Todd Hanley."

"Todd Hanley," the deputy repeated with a puzzled look. "How do you know this fella, Hanley, was one of them?"

"Because I killed him," Cole said in a matter of fact tone. "Might have killed one or two others too, but we didn't stick around to find out."

"Where exactly did it happen?" the deputy asked with an astonished look.

"Between the Telluride turn off and Sawpit."

"And you say the bodies are still out there?"

"Like I said, we didn't stay around to check on the ones that were up in the rocks, but we hid Todd Hanley's body in the rocks just a little ways off the road."

"Well, as soon as the sheriff gets back, I'm sure he'll want to ride out there and recover the bodies. We'll probably need you to ride along to show us where it happened. So, I'm gonna need you to stay around town for a while and that goes for the men you were with, too."

"You won't need me to show you where it happened," Cole replied. "They killed one of our mules and we left it right there in the road. But, we weren't planning on leaving town until tomorrow, anyway. So, I'll be glad to ride along if you'd prefer. But if you don't mind, I'd like to meet up with the other two men that are with me and let them know."

"Okay, where can I find you?"

"I'll be at the Yellow Canary Saloon," Cole replied.

"Alright, I'll come get you as soon as the sheriff gets back."

Cole nodded and then left the sheriff's office. When Cole got to the Yellow Canary Saloon, he paused just inside the door to look for Rusty and Clyde. There were only a few dozen men in the saloon, so Cole quickly determined Rusty and Clyde were not there and he continued to the bar. Although Cole didn't realize it, Drew Williams, Bart Taylor and the other two men that survived their attempt to hijack the whiskey wagons were sitting at a table in the corner.

"Take a look at that man with the fancy Winchester, Bart. Does he look familiar?"

"Not really," Bart Taylor replied.

"You sure? I'm thinking he might be one of those men with the whiskey wagons."

"Hard to say, Drew," Taylor said as he took another look at Cole.

"What about the rest of you? Does the man that just walked up to the bar look familiar?"

"He's dressed the same as that shooter on the second wagon, but he was too far away to say for sure," Brock replied.

"Well one thing's for sure, he ain't just some ordinary saddle bum. Not with a fancy rifle like that," Williams said as he continued staring at Cole. "You fellas stay here while I try to find out more about him."

Cole had just ordered a shot of whiskey from the bartender, when Drew Williams came up beside him.

"That'll be a dollar," the bartender said as he set Cole's shot of whiskey on the bar.

"A dollar!" Cole repeated with a surprised look.

"That's the goin' price," the bartender replied. "Hard as whiskey is to come by, you aughta be glad it ain't more."

"Remind me to order the cheap stuff next time," Cole replied.

"That is the cheap stuff," the bartender laughed.

"I guess whiskey really is worth its weight in gold," Cole chuckled as he reached into his pocket and put a silver dollar on the bar.

"How about you, mister? What'll you have?" the bartender asked looking at Drew Williams.

"I'll have a shot of the same," Williams said as he flipped the bartender a silver dollar.

"I gather by your reaction to the price of whiskey that you must be new to Telluride," Williams said to Cole as the bartender turned his attention to customers further down the bar.

"Matter of fact I just rolled into town a little while ago," Cole replied after taking a sip of his whiskey.

"Where you from?"

"Kansas originally."

"Must have been a long trip," Williams replied. "How long did it take you?"

"Well, I didn't mean I came here directly from Kansas," Cole explained. "I left Kansas a long time ago."

"Oh, I see," Williams said with a mock smile. "What brings you to Telluride?"

"I brought a load of freight over from Ridgeway."

"What were you hauling?"

"Whiskey," Cole replied in a matter of fact tone.

"I hear that can be dangerous," Williams replied trying to remain expressionless. "Did you have any trouble?"

"A little bit, but we made it here alright."

"I couldn't help noticing that fancy rifle you got there," Williams said pointing at Cole's rifle that was leaning against the bar. "I bet it's a real good shooter."

"Yeah, it's a real tack driver, alright," Cole replied in a friendly tone.

"Well, it was good talking to you, friend," Williams said after he emptied his glass. "By the way, I'm Drew Williams."

"I'm Cole Braxton."

"Good to meet you, Cole. Maybe we'll cross paths again," Williams said with a friendly smile.

Rusty and Clyde entered the saloon just as Drew Williams was walking away from Cole.

"Ain't that the same fellow that was talking to Todd Hanley in the saloon back in Placerville," Rusty asked when he spotted Williams walking away from Cole.

"I'm not sure. Things still look a little fuzzy," Clyde said, squinting his eyes.

"He sure looks like the same man," Rusty said with a curious look as he continued toward the bar.

When Williams saw Rusty and Clyde, he stopped short of the table where Bart Taylor, Pedro Martinez, and Brock Gilbert were still waiting. Williams looked away hoping that Rusty and Clyde would not notice him and then he motioned to Bart and the others to follow him as he headed for the door.

"Well, what about it? Was he one of them?" Bart asked once he and the others met Williams outside.

"Yeah, he was one of 'em, alright! His name is Cole Braxton," Williams replied.

"That's all I needed to know," Taylor said in an angry voice as he started back inside.

40

"Where do you think you're going?" Williams asked as he grabbed Bart's arm.

"I'm goin' in there and kill the bastard for what he did to Jack and my brother!" Taylor said with fire in his eyes.

"Don't be stupid. Didn't you see those two Texans just walk in?" Williams said. "Even if you could take Braxton, you'd never get all three of them."

"I didn't see the other two. I guess I was too busy watching the man at the bar," Taylor replied.

"Was Hanley with 'em?" Brock asked.

"No, but I'd sure like to find him! I got a bone to pick with that yellow bellied snake," Williams replied in an angry voice.

"You ain't the only one," Taylor said. "Once the shooting started, I'd like to know why he didn't just shoot those three."

"Well, what are we gonna do now?" Brock asked.

"I say we wait until the three of them walk out of the saloon and finish 'em off," Taylor said still showing his anger.

"Alright Bart, why don't you and Pedro go across the street. Brock and me will hide out in the alley at the end of the block. As soon as it's over, get out of town and meet back at the Ophir hideout.

***

Inside the saloon, Cole was trying to stretch his shot of whiskey when Rusty and Clyde joined him at the bar.

"How's the head," Cole asked.

"It still feels pretty thick," Clyde replied as he tugged at the thick bandage wrapped around his head.

"What did the doctor say?"

"He said I got something called a concoction."

"You mean a concussion," Cole chuckled.

"Well whatever it is, he said I should be fine in a day or two."

"He also said to stay away from whiskey for a few days," Rusty added with a big grin.

"It's just as well," Cole said smiling. "Whiskey is a buck a shot."

"You don't say!" Clyde said with a shocked look. "That's damn near the cost of a whole bottle of Black Panther."

"Black Panther! You call that whiskey? Hell, that ain't whiskey! A fellar told me that stuff was made with rubbing alcohol, pepper juice, and rattlesnake heads," Rusty said with an irritated look.

"Well, you sure drank plenty of it when we was chasing those mustangs through them canyons in Utah!" Clyde argued.

"Sounds like you fellows are lucky you didn't go blind drinking that stuff!" Cole laughed.

"It was the only way I could tolerate being with Clyde for all those months," Rusty laughed.

"Well, you gotta admit, it tasted pretty good at the time," Clyde said with a big grin.

"By the way Cole, who was that fellar you was talking to?" Rusty asked, ready to change the subject.

"What'll you fellas have to drink?" the bartender asked as he returned to Cole's end of the bar.

"At a dollar a shot, I'm afraid all we can afford is water," Rusty replied.

"It's like I already told this fella," the bartender said, pointing at Cole. "As hard as whisky is to come by ... you're lucky it ain't more!"

"Hell, we just brought two wagons full of the stuff to town!" Clyde said grinning. "So it should be a whole lot easier to come by now!"

"You fellas work for Joe Putra?" the bartender asked.

"No, we work for Nicholas Grant," Clyde replied.

"You ain't serious?" the bartender asked with a sudden sparkle in his eyes.

"Hell if I ain't! What you got against Nicholas Grant?" Clyde asked in a defensive tone.

"Not a thing, friend. It's just that Grant hasn't been able to get a shipment of whiskey through for weeks."

"Well, I'm tellin' you straight. We just brought two wagons full of whiskey over from Ridgeway," Rusty said with a proud expression.

"Hey fellas, these three men just brought two wagon loads of whiskey over from Ridgeway!" the bartender announced loudly.

The bar erupted in cheers and applause with a few of the men that were close by patting Cole, Rusty, and Clyde on the back.

"Sounds like you boys just became local heroes," a woman with a distinct southern accent said as she walked up to the bar next to Cole.

"I wouldn't consider hauling whiskey very heroic," Cole chuckled as he removed his hat and quickly looked the woman over.

She was an attractive woman, taller than most, with auburn hair, and a shapely figure. Her facial features were soft and pleasant to look at. Although at the time, they were altered by what Cole liked to call, war paint.

"You sound like you're from our neck of the woods," Rusty said with a big smile.

"They call me Dallas, if that gives you a clue," the woman said still smiling. "I own this joint!"

"Me and Clyde are from down along the Pecos," Rusty said as his eyes wandered up and down the woman several times.

"How about you, handsome, where are you from?" Dallas asked in a flirting voice as she looked at Cole.

"I'm from Kansas."

"Well Kansas, sounds like I owe you and your side kicks a favor," Dallas said. Then in a louder voice she said to the bartender, "Give our friends a round on the house, Sam!"

"Will do, Dallas," Sam replied.

"Thank you kindly, Dallas," Rusty said smiling.

"You're welcome, come back and see me anytime," Dallas said winking at Cole and walking away.

"Wish I could see Joe Putra's face when he finds out you fellas just brought two wagon loads of whiskey to town," Sam, the bartender, said as he put glasses in front of Rusty and Clyde.

"Who is Joe Putra, anyway?" Cole asked.

"He's a whiskey supplier," Sam said as he filled the three glasses.

Rusty downed his shot of whiskey and immediately reached for the one in front of Clyde, but Clyde managed to grab it first.

"Don't you remember what the doctor said, Clyde?" Rusty asked quickly.

"I guess that thump on the head must have gave me amnesty!" Clyde replied with a big grin just before downing the whiskey.

"You mean amnesia," Cole chuckled after emptying his own glass. Then looking at Sam he said, "This fella Joe Putra...I guess he must be in competition with Nicholas Grant, then."

"Yeah, that's right."

"I take it he and Nicholas don't get along, then."

"I don't know as how there are any hard feelings between Grant and Putra, but since Grant's prices are about half of what Joe Putra charges, I can't imagine they're the best of friends."

"Sounds like Joe Putra needs to lower his prices," Cole said.

"Well, according to Joe Putra, he can't afford to on account of the extra money he pays for guards and the fact that he has to haul his whiskey all the way from Dolores. Which may be true, but the fact is, he also adds a little water to his whiskey and don't think my customers don't know it, too...especially the Irish."

43

"Doesn't sound like this fellow, Putra is a very popular man around Telluride," Cole chuckled.

"Mister, the only friends Joe Putra has in Telluride or anywhere else for that matter, are the ones he's bought and paid for. I know one thing for sure, all the saloons in town would rather buy their whiskey from Grant."

When Cole heard Dallas say, "Good afternoon, Sheriff," he turned around and saw Deputy Wallace and another man walking toward the bar.

"Mister Braxton, this is Sheriff Douglas," Deputy Wallace said as he and the sheriff approached Cole.

"Nice to meet you, Sheriff. This is Rusty Gibb and that's Clyde Decker," Cole said. "These are the men that were with me when we were bushwhacked."

"What happened to your head, Mister Decker?" the sheriff asked Clyde.

"A double crossing pole cat named Todd Hanley, beaned me on the head with the butt of his pistol when I wasn't looking," Clyde replied.

"Todd Hanley was the man that Mister Braxton shot," Deputy Wallace explained.

"Is that how you figured out he was working with the men that ambushed you?" the sheriff asked.

"That was part of it," Cole said. "You see Hanley originally called us over to his wagon saying that Clyde had been shot. Then when we got there, he pulled a gun on us."

"Yeah, but Cole tricked him and shot the son of a bitch!" Rusty said with a big grin.

"I understand you might have killed a few others as well," the sheriff said looking Cole in eyes.

"I'm pretty sure I got one or two others, but I might have just winged 'em," Cole replied. "Like I told Deputy Wallace...we didn't stick around to find out for sure."

"Well Mister Braxton, what do you say we ride out there and take a look?"

"Fine by me," Cole replied. "I'll need to borrow a horse."

"That won't be necessary. My other deputy is waiting for us over at the jail with a wagon," the sheriff said. "I figured we might as well bring back the bodies while we're at it. So, you can just ride along with him."

"What about me and Clyde?" Rusty asked. "You need us to tag along, too?"

"No thanks fellas. I think we can handle it, alright."

"While I'm gone, why don't you two go get our things from the wagons and check into a hotel?" Cole suggested.

"The Sheridan Hotel right up the street is as good as any," Deputy Wallace said.

"Okay...but...uh...you didn't forget we ain't got no money, did you Cole?"

"Matter of fact I did, Rusty," Cole said as he reached into his pocket and then handed Rusty several bills. "That aughta be enough for a couple rooms. I'll catch up with you at the hotel and we'll grab a bite to eat as soon as I get back."

"Okay Cole, we'll see you later," Rusty said as he and Clyde turned to leave.

Although Drew Williams and the rest of his gang were originally planning to ambush Cole, Clyde, and Rusty as they walked out of the saloon, when they saw the sheriff and Deputy Wallace enter the saloon they quickly abandoned their plan and disappeared down the alleys.

# Chapter Five

As Cole, the sheriff, and his two deputies were nearing the ambush sight, the horses sensed something that made them very uncomfortable and it took the sheriff and his men quite a bit of effort to maintain control of their mounts. The reason for the horses' bad behavior became quite evident as the men cleared the trees and spotted a large bear dragging what was left of the dead mule off the road. Deputy Wallace fired a couple of shots into the air and the bear reluctantly left the mule and scampered down the steep slope.

"Best keep your rifles handy while we're here in case that bear comes back," the sheriff warned loudly. Then looking at Cole he asked, "Mister Braxton, where abouts were those men when they ambushed you."

"They were up in that outcropping," Cole said as he pointed up the slope.

"Alright Amos, go ahead and keep the wagon here," the sheriff said to the deputy that was driving the wagon. "The road's too narrow to turn the wagon around up ahead, anyway," then to Deputy Wallace he said, "Jared, tie your horse to the wagon. Then go up into those rocks and see if you can find anything."

"Okay, Russ," Jared replied.

"Mister Braxton, why don't you show me where you hid Hanley's body?"

Cole and the sheriff cautiously walked down the road with their rifles ready and on the constant lookout for the bear. Once they reached the large pool of dried blood in the road which marked the exact spot where the mule had originally gone down, Cole led the sheriff off the road on the uphill side. Hanley's body was not visible from the road, but Cole quickly spotted the stacked rocks that he and Rusty set up to mark the spot where they had hidden the body.

"There you are, Sheriff," Cole said pointing between the rocks.

"I've seen this man's mug before," the sheriff said as he took a close look at Hanley's face. "But, I'm pretty sure his name isn't Hanley. How'd you get hooked up with him, anyway?"

"Nicholas Grant hired him as a guard. According to Nicholas, he was an ex-lawman."

"Maybe, that's why he looks familiar, but the name Hanley sure don't seem right," the sheriff said, trying to search his memory. "Terrible thing when an ex-lawman goes bad. Well....give me a hand, Mister Braxton and we'll carry him back to the road. Jared and Amos can help us carry him back to the wagon after we check for other bodies."

After leaning their rifles against a large boulder, Cole and the sheriff pulled Hanley's body out of the rocks and carried it to the road. They were going back for their rifles when Jared shouted from the outcropping, "Hey Russell...I got two bodies up here!"

"I guess you were right, Mister Braxton," the sheriff said. "Sounds like you did get two more of 'em."

"Yeah, I thought so," Cole said without any emotions.

"Okay Jared, stay put and we'll make our way up there," the sheriff yelled to the deputy.

Once Jared waved to acknowledge that he heard the sheriff's instructions, the sheriff and Cole retrieved their rifles and started making their way up the slope toward the outcropping.

"If we're lucky, we'll be able to recognize those other bodies and maybe, it'll give us a clue as to who the rest of the gang might be," the sheriff said breathing heavily. "Just how many men were there, anyway?"

"It was hard to tell exactly because they were pretty well hidden in the rocks, but I'm guessing there were at least five or six."

"So that would make it six or seven including Hanley," the sheriff said while stopping to catch his breath. "I sure wish I could remember Hanley's real name?"

"Maybe, the marshal in Ridgeway can help you out," Cole said as he also paused to catch his breath.

"Yeah, maybe. Where exactly were you when you shot those men?" the sheriff asked.

"About another fifty yards further down the road," Cole replied as he pointed.

"You must be a hell of a shot!" the sheriff replied with an impressed expression.

"I'm better than most, I guess," Cole replied trying not to sound like he was bragging.

"I'll say!" the sheriff replied looking at Cole. "Where did you learn to shoot like that?"

"Been shootin' ever since I was tall enough to pour powder down the barrel of a musket," Cole replied smiling.

47

"I been meaning to ask you about that fancy rifle you got. I imagine you paid a pretty penny for it."

"It was given to me as a gift," Cole replied.

"Hell of a gift," the sheriff said looking at Cole with a surprised expression.

"Yeah, I thought so."

"Mind if I ask what you did to deserve a gift like that?"

"I guess you'd have to ask the man that gave it to me."

"And who would that be?"

"Ever hear of William Cody?"

"Buffalo Bill Cody?" the sheriff asked with a stunned look.

"Yep, that's him," Cole replied.

After hearing Cole's reply, sheriff remained silent until they reached Jared. When he and Cole reached Jared, the sheriff moved from corpse to corpse to see if he could recognize either of the bodies.

"That rifle of yours sure did a number on 'em," the sheriff said after seeing that both men had been shot in the head with little remaining of their faces.

"Didn't have time to pick my shots, Sheriff. I shot at whatever I could see," Cole replied.

"I understand," the sheriff replied as he bent down and picked up the dead man's Winchester and a couple of spent cartridges. "Looks like they were both using 44-40s."

"Yeah, I guess we were lucky they weren't armed with something more powerful," Cole replied.

"Well, once we get the bodies down to the wagon, we'll go through their pockets. Maybe we'll find something that will give us a clue as to who they are."

The three men left their rifles and picked up the first of the two bodies. Because of the steep and rough terrain, it took them quite a while to negotiate their way down to the wagon. After a brief rest, they returned for the second body and then they retrieved Todd Hanley's body last. When all three of the bodies were in the bed of the wagon, Jared and Amos went through their pockets while Cole and the sheriff went back up into the rocks for the rifles.

"Were you serious when you said Buffalo Bill Cody gave you that rifle?" the sheriff asked as he and Cole were making their way back down to the wagon with the rifles.

"Yep."

"How did you come to know him?'

"I was in his Wild West Show."

"Is that right? Well, I'll be damned. I guess that vouches for your shooting ability," the sheriff said. "I saw his show a few months ago when I was in St. Louis. But seems to me, his top shooter was a young girl. I think her name was Oakley."

"Yeah, Annie Oakley is her name. She joined the show after I left."

"How come you left?"

"Got tired of being on the go all the time, mostly," Cole replied. "I guess the final straw was when Bill started talking about taking the show all the way over to England and touring all over Europe."

"That sounds pretty exciting to me."

"Yeah, except for the part about crossing the Atlantic Ocean. I can't imagine being stuck on a boat for a week," Cole chuckled. "And to be honest, the thought of getting stuck out there in the middle of the ocean somewhere... made me a little nervous. Back in Kansas about the only swimming I ever did...was in a horse trough on bath day."

"At least you can swim," the sheriff laughed. "I never learned myself. Never had a reason to."

"It's never too late to learn. My older brother never learned until he was a full growed man."

"Tell me something, Mister Braxton, what are you and your partners gonna do next?"

"Come tomorrow, I guess the three of us will drive those wagons back over to Ridgeway."

"And then what?"

"I'm not sure about Rusty and Clyde. I think they're set on going back to Texas. But, I plan on staying in Ridgeway until Nicholas is ready to send another load of whiskey over to Telluride."

"So, you plan on continuing to work for Nicholas Grant?"

"Might as well. The job pays good and I got nothing else lined up."

"Well, I got a proposition for you. How would you and your partners like to make some money on the way back to Ridgeway?"

"Doing what?"

"Hauling gold and silver," the sheriff said. "You're headed that way anyway and your wagons will be empty, so why not take the opportunity to make a little money?"

"Well for one thing, the wagons and teams aren't ours. They belong to Nicholas Grant."

"I'm aware of that, but don't you worry about Nicholas. He'll be paid a fair price for one day's use of his wagons and mules," the sheriff said. "And I think I know Nicholas Grant well enough to say he's never objected to making money."

49

"Well...I don't know. Hauling gold and silver sounds like pretty risky business."

"So is hauling whiskey," the sheriff laughed.

"I guess you got a point there," Cole admitted with a short chuckle. "Tell me a little more about the job."

"Alright... as you know, Telluride is a mining town. Most of the big mines around Telluride produce silver mostly, but they also produce a little gold and the bank in Telluride serves as a gold exchange for all the small time miners and prospectors. So, twice a month, me and my two deputies escort a shipment of silver bound for the mint in Denver along with all the gold, the bank has on hand, to the train depot in Ridgeway. Neil Morton, the bank manager, normally takes care of the arrangements for the wagons and drivers with one of the local freight companies and I just worry about guarding the shipment. But after all the robberies we've had lately, I'd feel a whole lot better with a couple of men that know how to handle themselves on those wagons instead of ordinary freighters. In other words, Mister Braxton... I'd like to see you and your partners on those wagons and I'm sure if I talk to Mister Morton, he'll have no objections.

"What does the job pay?"

"I believe Mister Morton normally pays the freight company four hundred dollars."

"Well, I'm interested, but I can't speak for Rusty or Clyde. So, I'll leave the final decision up to them."

When Cole and the sheriff reached the wagon, they looked over the items that Jared and Amos discovered in the pockets of the three men which amounted to eighteen dollars, some change, two cheap watches, some tobacco, rolling paper, and matches.

"Not much to show for three men's lives," the sheriff commented.

"This one was wearing that fancy hand tooled holster rig with the initials M T on it, Russell," Jared said as he held up the holster rig for the sheriff to see. "The other holsters were just plain."

"Well, that ain't much of a clue, but it's something," the sheriff replied. "I'll get the newspaper to run a list of their belongings in next week's paper. Maybe, some next of kin will come forward to claim their effects and at least we'll find out who these fellas are."

After covering the bodies with a canvas tarp, Cole and Amos climbed up on the wagon seat and once Jared and the sheriff were mounted, they started back toward Telluride.

It was after sundown and the remnants of daylight were fading fast when they reached the edge of town.

"Hold up there a minute, Amos," the sheriff said loudly when they reached the jail.

Amos pulled the team to a stop and the sheriff reined his horse up next to Cole's side of the wagon.

"I appreciate you riding out with us to collect the bodies, Mister Braxton," the sheriff said. "I'm gonna leave you now to finish up a few things in the office, before I go on home for supper. I'd like you to consider what we talked about earlier and talk to your partners about it. I usually make my rounds around nine o'clock. I'll stop by your hotel room to get your answer."

"Okay Sheriff, I'll see you around nine."

Amos started the team and after dropping Cole off at the hotel, he continued on to the undertaker to drop off the three bodies.

"Can I help you, Sir?" the hotel desk clerk asked Cole as he walked up to the registration counter.

"I'm Cole Braxton. I believe my partners stopped in earlier and got us some rooms."

"Yes sir, Mister Braxton. You'll be in room 203. Mister Gibb and Mister Decker are right across the hall in room 204," the clerk said as he laid a key to Cole's room on the counter. "I took the liberty of having your bag put in your room."

"Thanks, I appreciate that," Cole said as he reached into his pocket and placed a quarter on the counter.

When Cole opened the door to his room he was somewhat surprised by the decor and furnishings which were quite elegant. He laid his Winchester on the bed and then walked across the hall.

"Who is it?" Rusty asked after Cole knocked on the door.

"It's me, Cole."

"Howdy Cole," Rusty said as he pulled open the door. "Have you checked out your room yet?"

"Yeah, I'm right across the hall."

"These rooms are mighty fancy, ain't they?"

"Fanciest room I ever slept in!" Clyde said from across the room. "And the beds are real soft too."

"Well, you fellas want to get a bite to eat?"

"You bet!" Rusty said in an enthusiastic voice. "If I don't put somthin' in my stomach soon, it's liable start gnawin' on my back bone."

The three men walked down stairs and considered eating in the dining room, but when they noticed how the other diners were dressed; they opted for a less formal setting and walked a few blocks to a small café.

"You find Hanley's body, alright?" Rusty asked after the waitress walked away to place their orders.

"Yeah, there was a big old bear trying to drag that dead mule off, but Hanley's body was right where we left it and we found two more up in the rocks."

"I been meanin' to tell you...that sure was some mighty good shootin' you done back there," Rusty said. "I always thought me and Clyde was good shots, but we ain't nothin' compared to you."

"Well, thanks. I guess if you practice long enough you can get good at anything."

"Maybe so, but you still gots to have some natural ability to start with," Clyde said. "Back home on the Pecos, most of the fellas was purty good with a rifle, but me and Rusty could still outshoot every one of 'em on account of our natural ability."

"Well, there's a lot to be said for natural ability," Cole agreed.

"I imagine you must have done a lot of shootin' during the war," Rusty said.

"Yeah, unfortunately I did," Cole replied in a modest and somber tone.

"Me and Clyde was with Hood's Texas Brigade."

"That was a fine unit, alright. You fellas aughta be proud."

"It's good of you to say," Rusty said with an appreciative smile.

"What unit was you with, Cole?" Clyde asked.

"I started with the 14th Misouri Volunteers, but I was reassigned to Berdan's Sharpshooters."

"I've heard of them," Rusty said.

"Me too. Wasn't they some kind of assassins?" Clyde asked with a shocked look.

"We weren't assassins," Cole said in a defensive voice. "We were sharpshooters and snipers. Granted, our job was to pick off the Confederate officers. But, that was just strategy. Once you eliminate the leaders, a battle turns into a brawl and it becomes every man for himself with no real united objective...or at least that's what Colonel Berdan always said."

"I suppose that be the truth," Rusty said. "Anyway, your shootin' ability sure came in handy today."

"You fellas did your part, too," Cole said. "Which reminds me...the sheriff wants to know if we would be interested in making some money on our way back to Ridgeway?"

"Hell, yeah we're interested!" Clyde said.

"Not so fast, Clyde!" Rusty said with an annoyed expression. "How do you know we're interested? Cole ain't told us what we gotta do yet."

"Well, if the sheriff is involved, it can't be nothin' illegal. So, why wouldn't we be interested in making some money?"

"Just because it ain't illegal, don't mean I'd be interested. For all you know the job might be herdin' a bunch of sheep across the mountains!"

"That don't make no sense, Rusty!" Clyde replied in an irritated tone. "What would the sheriff be doin' with a herd of sheep?"

"That ain't the point, Clyde! The point is... there's some jobs I wouldn't be interested in!"

"Rusty's right, Clyde," Cole chuckled. "Let me tell you what the job is and then you can decide if you're interested."

"Okay, fine," Clyde replied, with a pouty frown.

"Twice a month the sheriff and his two deputies escort a shipment of gold and silver to the train depot in Ridgeway and since we'll be taking the wagons back to Ridgeway, anyhow...he wondered if we would be interested in hauling the gold and silver."

"How much does the job pay?" Clyde asked.

"What difference does it make?" Rusty snapped with a sarcastic grin. "You already said you was interested!"

"I am, but there ain't nothing wrong with finding out how much the job pays!" Clyde argued.

"See there... that's what I'm talking about! For all you know the job might only pay a dollar and you already said you was interested instead of waiting to find out just how much the job does pay!" Rusty said in a heated voice with a satisfied smile.

"The job pays four hundred dollars," Cole interjected, smiling.

"Four hundred dollars!" Rusty repeated with a surprised and excited look.

"Yeah but, it isn't all ours," Cole said still smiling. "Nicholas Grant is entitled to some of the money for the use of his wagons and mules."

"How much do you figure will be left over for us?" Rusty asked.

"I reckon that depends on Nicholas, but I'm sure he'll be fair with us. Especially, since we're the ones taking the risk. So... I imagine we might be looking at around a hundred dollars apiece."

"Well, for a hundred dollars...hell yes, I'm interested!" Rusty said.

"See there, I told you we was interested!" Clyde replied with a big grin.

Before Rusty could counter, the waitress returned with their order and the men's attention quickly turned to the food on her tray. When they finished their supper, Cole paid the bill and left the waitress a quarter to show his appreciation for her prompt and attentive service.

Cole had just removed his boots and was lying on the bed when the sheriff knocked on the door to his room. Cole instinctively reached for his pistol as he rolled off the bed and then tossed it back on the bed once he found out it was the sheriff at the door.

"Good evening, Mister Braxton," the sheriff said as Cole opened the door.

"Evening Sheriff, come on in."

"I won't stay long. I was just wondering if you had an answer for me."

"Yeah, I talked to Clyde and Rusty and we'd like to take you up on your offer."

"Good, I was hoping that would be the case," the sheriff said with a big smile. "I already talked to Mister Morton at the bank and after hearing about today's events, he was very agreeable to hiring you and your partners."

"So, what's the plan, Sheriff?"

"In the past, the freighters have met me and my deputies at the bank by eight o'clock in the morning. Mister Morton generally gets there right at eight o'clock sharp and after he gets the vault open, the freighters load the wagons while me and my deputies stand guard. Then once the wagons are loaded we head out. I figured on having Amos ride on one of the wagons while me and Jared take the lead on horseback. Once we get to Sawpit, we'll lock the gold and silver in the bank overnight and then continue to Ridgeway the following morning."

"Okay Sheriff, we'll see you at the bank by eight."

"Call me Russell," the sheriff said as he extended his hand.

"Okay Russell, my first name's Cole and my partners are Rusty and Clyde," Cole said as he shook Russell's hand.

# Chapter Six

After abandoning their plans to ambush Cole, Rusty, and Clyde as they were leaving the saloon, Drew Williams headed for Ridgeway while Bart Taylor and the rest of the gang left Telluride and rode to their hideout near Ophir. When Drew Williams reached Placerville, he stopped to get a bite to eat and then continued to Ridgeway. It was late in the evening by the time Williams reached Ridgeway and he was sure Jonas Bradley would no longer be at his office, so Williams rode to Bradley's house.

"What the hell are you doing here? I told you never to come to my house!" Jonas Bradley said when he answered the door and saw Drew Williams.

"I know, but I figured it was important enough that I needed to see you right away!" Williams replied in a flustered voice.

"Who is it, dear?" Bradley's wife asked loudly from the kitchen.

"Just a man with a note from Mike Fish. He needs me at the office, but I won't be long," Bradley replied.

Bradley grabbed his hat from the coat rack and ushered Williams off the porch.

"Alright, what's so important?" Bradley asked in an angry voice.

"Things went bad today," Williams replied.

"What happened?" Bradley snapped.

"Everything went wrong. First of all, there were two wagons not just one. So, we had two drivers and a guard to contend with instead of just one driver. And the guard on the second wagon turned out to be a hell of a shot. He ended up killing Bart's brother and Jack Daniels. So, we had to turn back."

"What about Todd Hanley? Why didn't he just kill that guard?"

"I don't know what happened to Hanley. I guess the son of a bitch must have chickened out! We haven't seen hide nor hair of him since we tried to take the wagons."

"You mean the whiskey shipment got through to Telluride?" Bradley asked with a concerned look.

"Yeah, there wasn't anything we could do to stop it."

"Damn it! I'll bet Joe Putra is furious!" Bradley said looking even more worried.

"Sorry Boss," Williams apologized.

"Alright, come by the jail tomorrow morning after my deputy has left and we'll figure out what to do next."

The next morning Drew Williams met Marshal Jonas Bradley in his office shortly after Deputy Mike Fish left to go home and catch a few hours of sleep. The marshal's expression showed his anger as Williams proceeded to lay out the exact details of what had occurred during the botched hijacking.

"Alright, they got lucky!" Bradley said in a heated voice.

"So, what now, Boss?" Williams asked.

"Grant will probably be pretty cocky now that he got a shipment through," Bradley said. "Which probably means he'll try it again just as soon as those men get back with his wagons."

"How we gonna stop 'em with only four of us left?" Williams asked.

"That's your problem!" Bradley said in an angry voice. "Hire more men!"

"That may not be as easy as it sounds, Boss. Especially once word gets out that two of our men got killed during this last attempt."

"Well, we can't afford to let another shipment get through. Joe Putra will be madder than a wet cat as it is!" Bradley said. "Maybe we need to figure out how to get rid of that fella with the fancy Winchester. What did you say his name was?"

"Cole Braxton," Williams replied.

"Alright, I'll talk to Grant to see if I can find out more about Braxton and I'll also try to find out when he's planning on sending out another shipment."

"What do you want me to do, Boss?"

"You better head over to Placerville. You can try to hire some more men and be there in case Grant tries to slip another shipment through."

\*\*\*

When Cole, Rusty, and Clyde arrived at the bank, Sheriff Russell Douglas and his two deputies, Jared Walters and Amos Crabtree, were waiting. The bank manager, Neil Morton, arrived at exactly eight o'clock and after the sheriff took care of the introductions, Mister Morton opened the vault. Russell and his deputies stood guard while Cole, Rusty, and Clyde used a special cart to transfer the silver ingots and bags of gold dust to the wagons through a side door. The gold and silver was divided equally between the two wagons and then covered with tarps. Amos tied his horse to the tailgate of Clyde's wagon and climbed up next to Clyde on the first wagon. Cole and Rusty climbed up onto the second wagon and once Russell and Jared were mounted, the procession started for Ridgeway with Russell and Jared staying a short distance ahead of the

56

wagons acting more or less like scouts. When they approached the open stretch of road where they had previously seen the bear, they slowed their horses and pulled their rifles. But when they broke through the trees, the road ahead was clear with no sight of the bear or the mule carcass.

It was midafternoon by the time the wagons reached Placerville. The men proceeded directly to the First Bank of Placerville which had an enormous vault considering the size of the community. Russell and his deputies stood guard while Cole, Rusty, and Clyde used carts to transfer the silver and gold into the vault. Once the wagons were empty, Russell and Jared rode to the livery with the rest of the men following in the wagons. After making arrangements to have the animals watered and fed, the men unsaddled the horses and unhitched the mules. Then they walked to the Placerville Palace Hotel and Saloon. Due to the limited number of rooms available in the hotel, the house rules required all male guests to sleep two to a room in order to accommodate more guests. So, Rusty and Clyde shared one room. Russell's deputies shared another and Cole shared a third room with Russell. After stowing their rifles and extra gear in their rooms, the men met in the saloon. With the first leg of the trip behind them, spirits were high and the men were ready to let off a little steam. After establishing that the price of whiskey was a reasonable two bits a shot, Cole bought the first round of drinks and Russell bought the second.

"There's that man again," Rusty said as he noticed Drew Williams pass by the bar room and enter the dining hall.

"What man are you talking about?" Cole asked.

"That man I saw you talking to when me and Clyde walked into the Yellow Canary Saloon back in Telluride."

"So it is," Cole said after glancing at the man. "I think he said his name was Drew or something like that."

"That's the same man me and Clyde saw talkin' to Todd Hanley last time we were in here."

"I wish you would have mentioned that when we were in Telluride," Cole said as he took another look at the man.

"Well if I recall, I asked you about him, but then we got side tracked talking about the price of whiskey."

"Hey Russell," Cole said in a loud voice as he motioned to the sheriff who was standing on the other side of his deputies.

"Yeah, what's up?" Russell asked as he walked closer to Cole.

"See that man sitting in the dining hall with the black hat? Rusty says he saw him talking to Todd Hanley last time we were here, which was the day before we were bushwhacked."

"Are you sure?" the Sheriff asked as he continued looking at the man.

"Yeah, I'm sure," Rusty replied. Then turning to Clyde he asked, "Hey Clyde, ain't that the same man we saw talkin' to Hanley last time we was in here?"

"Yep, that's one of 'em," Clyde replied.

"How many were there?" Cole asked with another surprised look.

"There was that one and one other one," Rusty said. "We started to say howdy to Hanley, but by the time we finished our supper, Hanley the two men he was with was all gone."

"Funny thing is...Rusty and Clyde saw him here the night before we were bushwhacked and I saw him in Telluride a few hours after we were bushwhacked."

"Yeah, I've seen him around Telluride a few times myself," Russell replied. "Maybe, I aughta go have a talk with him."

"Mind if I tag along?" Cole asked.

"Not at all," Russell replied.

Drew Williams had just finished placing his order with the waitress when he noticed Cole and Russell walking toward his table. His first reaction was to slowly drop his right hand into his lap and pull his pistol, but Williams was a very accomplished liar and conman. So instead of pulling his pistol, Williams sported a large smile as he stood up extending his hand and said, "Cole Braxton isn't it?"

"That's right," Cole said as he reluctantly took Williams' hand and shook it.

"I rarely forget a face and I told you our paths would probably cross again," Williams said in a jovial tone.

"This is Sheriff Douglas," Cole said motioning toward Russell.

"Yes of course...I recognize our fine sheriff, but I've never had the pleasure," Williams said with a warm smile as he extended his hand to Russell. "I'm Drew Williams, Sheriff. Can I buy you gentleman a drink?"

"Not for me, thanks," Russell said as he sat down.

"Me neither," Cole said as he also sat down.

"Well then, sit down won't you."

"Who did you share a room with last time you were here?" Russell asked getting right to the point.

"That's an unusual question, Sheriff," Williams replied. "Mind if I ask why you want to know?"

"I'd rather you just answer the question," Russell said.

"Alright, as a matter of fact I generally get a room all to myself. I know all about the house rule requiring two men to a room, but because I'm a regular here the manager and I have an agreement."

"What do you know about a man named, Todd Hanley?" Russell asked

"Todd Hanley," Williams repeated while doing a good job of showing no emotions. "I don't believe I know the man."

"I thought you said you never forget a face?" Russell said quickly staring Williams in the eyes. "You were seen right here in this very saloon talking to him."

"I said I rarely forget a face, Sheriff," Williams said trying to maintain his smile. "But now that you mentioned it...I do recall meeting the man a few days ago."

"Was that the first time you ever met him?" Russell asked.

"Yes, it was. As I recall he was with another man, but the other man never gave his name. I overheard them talking about some merchandise they had for sale and ...that being my line of work...buying and selling, that is...I introduced myself."

"What exactly did they have for sale?" Russell asked maintaining his suspicious stare.

"Well, we never actually got that far in our discussion. To be honest, Sherriff, they seemed very secretive and guarded. In fact, I almost got the feeling that they were involved in something dishonest. So, naturally... I excused myself and based on your questions, I suspect my suspicions may have been correct. And judging from Mister Braxton's presence...I'm guessing this Hanley character must have something to do with the attempted hijacking of that whiskey shipment that occurred a few days ago."

"Sounds like you got it all figured out, Mister Williams," Russell said.

"Everything except who was responsible for the attempted hold up," Williams said with a sly grin. "Which I assume is your next question."

"No... matter of fact, I was gonna ask you what exactly it is that you buy and sell," Russell asked with a slight grin.

"Anything and everything, Sherriff. If there's a profit to be made I'm interested!" Williams said with a soft laugh.

"Even whiskey?" Cole asked.

"Even whiskey...providing it's not stolen of course," Williams said looking Cole directly in the eyes.

"What about the fella Hanley was with? What did he look like?" Russell asked with a serious expression.

"Well now if I recall, he was about medium height with shaggy brown hair and a scruffy beard. He had on a faded tan shirt with dungarees and come to think of it... he wore a rather fancy tooled gun belt."

"That sounds sorta like one of those men whose bodies we recovered up in the rocks," Russell said glancing at Cole with just the slightest hint of excitement.

"Were there any initials on the gun belt?" Cole asked.

"Seems like there were, but I couldn't make them out," Williams said grinning again.

"Where exactly do you live, Mister Williams?" Russell asked in a tone that seemed a little less suspicious.

"Like I said Sherriff, I'm in the business of buying and selling. As a result, I hang my hat in half a dozen places from Ridgeway to Durango."

"Including Telluride," Russell said.

"Including Telluride," Drew Williams replied.

"Next time you're in Telluride...make sure you look me up, Mister Williams. Just in case I have some more questions for you," Russell said in a firm voice.

"Be my pleasure, Sheriff," Williams replied smiling again.

As Russell and Cole stood up, so did Williams and because he offered his hand, both Russell and Cole shook it even though they were reluctant to do so.

"What do you think, Russell?" Cole asked as they were walking back to the bar.

"He's a cagy one," Russell replied.

"Slimy was more the word I was thinking of," Cole chuckled.

"Yeah but, he gave me no reason to think he was involved in the ambush," Russell said with an uncertain look. "And that description he gave us of the man with Hanley sure sounds legit right down to the holster rig."

"The question is was that description based on his recollection from the night before or was it based on his recollection of the man when he was with him during the ambush?"

"The same question already crossed my mind, too," Russell admitted as they continued to the bar.

The following morning, Russell and Cole were up at first light. They dressed quickly and after ensuring their men were awake, they went down to the dining hall and drank black coffee until the others joined them. After a breakfast of black coffee, biscuits, and sausage gravy, Cole and Russell split the bill and the men went to the livery. The routine at the Placerville bank was much the same as the previous morning and once the wagons were loaded, they continued toward Ridgeway.

The second leg of the trip was also uneventful. Although due to the increased number of travelers they encountered on the road, each one a potential robber, all the men maintained a much higher state of alert. When they reached the rail yard in Ridgeway, Russell and his deputies along with two railroad express guards kept watch while Cole, Clyde, and Rusty helped four railroad employees unload the gold and silver into the railway express car.

"That does it, fellas! Good job!" Russell said loudly after getting a signed receipt.

"I believe I know a place where we could get a couple of free drinks if you men want follow us over to Nicholas Grant's Warehouse," Cole said.

"I think we'll take you up on that, Cole," Russell said looking as if someone had just lifted a heavy weight off his shoulders.

When the men arrived at the warehouse, Nicholas and all of his employees met them with cheers and applause.

"Welcome back, lads!" Nicholas said as they exchanged firm handshakes and he gave Cole, Rusty, and Clyde each a hearty pat on the back.

"Nicholas, this is Sheriff Douglas and these are his deputies, Jared Walters and Amos Crabtree," Cole said as Russell and his deputies dismounted.

"Aye, me and the sheriff have met before," Nicholas said as he shook Russell's hand.

"I hope you don't mind, but I invited them over for a drink."

"Splendid idea, Cole," Nicholas replied as he shook hands with Amos and Jared. Then in a loud voice he announced, "Everybody come inside, we have a little surprise celebration arranged for these fine lads!"

Inside the warehouse, a table had been set up with plates, forks, glasses, several bottles of Grant's standard whiskey, and two cakes. Grant's wife, who was stylishly outfitted from head to toe, and Julie Roberts, Grant's book keeper and only female employee, were standing behind the table ready to serve the cake.

"Gentlemen, before we get started I'd like to present my lovely wife, Clair," Nicholas said beaming with pride.

All of the men, except Cole, offered up a variety of courtesies with their hats in hand and after returning the same, Clair walked out from behind the table and gave Cole a warm hug.

"Clair is my sister," Cole said after a brief pause to savor the surprised expressions on everyone's faces.

After the room erupted in laughter, Clair returned to the table and started passing out cake while the men helped themselves to the liquid refreshments. After finishing second helpings of cake and whiskey, Rusty and Clyde walked over to Cole who was at the table refilling his own glass.

"Hey Cole, me and Clyde was wondering if you had a chance to talk to Nicholas about our share of the money for hauling the gold and silver."

"Not yet," Cole replied. "But it looks like he's coming this way. So, we can do it together right now."

"Are you enjoying yourselves, lads?" Nicholas asked in a booming voice.

"You bet we are," Clyde replied, smiling.

"It was real nice of you to throw this little shindig for us," Clyde added.

"Hey Nick, I got something I need to talk to you about," Cole said expressing his appreciation.

"Aye, if it's about your money, we can walk over to the bank as soon as we've had our fill of celebrating," Nicholas said with a broad smile.

"Thanks, but that's not what I wanted to talk to you about."

"Well, what is it then?

"I took the liberty of using your wagons and mules to haul a bunch of gold and silver over here from Telluride. I figured since we were coming this way anyhow, there wouldn't be any harm in it and the bank paid me four hundred dollars to do it."

"Aye, the sheriff already told me about it."

"Sorry, I guess I should have mentioned it earlier," Cole said somewhat surprised and embarassed. "Anyway, Rusty and Clyde were curious about their cut."

"What did you have in mind when you agreed to take on the job?"

"I figured after you took what was fair for the use of your wagons and mules, the three of us would split the rest," Cole replied.

"So you're leaving it up to me is that it?"

"They're your wagons and mules," Cole replied.

"You're an honorable man, Cole," Nicholas said as he gave Cole a hearty slap on the back. "And so are you lads," Nicholas added, looking at Rusty and Clyde. "You're all fine men! Now then...as you know, Cole has decided to continue working for me, but I was wondering what you lads plan on doing now that you've fulfilled your obligation."

"We was planning on continuing to Texas," Rusty replied.

"Aye, Texas. Well lads, Texas will still be there for a long time, so I was hoping I could talk you into making at least one more trip for me before you go. I'll pay you the same amount and as a bonus... I won't take a nickel out of that four hundred dollars from the bank...except maybe... the cost of that replacement mule I had to buy."

"When was you planning on sending out another shipment?" Rusty asked.

"I could have the wagons ready for another trip tomorrow morning!" Nicholas said with a sparkle in his eyes.

"What about another guard?" Rusty asked.

"As a matter of fact, I think I've just about convinced the sheriff and his two deputies to ride along with you," Nicholas replied.

"How about it, Clyde?" Rusty asked. "Russell and his deputies is all pretty good ole boys. I doubt we'll have any trouble with them along. So... I'm willing if you are?"

"Well I reckon it's like Nicholas said... Texas will still be there. Hell, we ain't been back for over twenty years. I reckon putting it off a little while longer won't make no difference," Clyde replied, grinning.

"Splendid!" Nicholas said with a pleased expression as he shook hands with Clyde and then Rusty. "Why don't you lads have another drink while Cole and I try to go finalize an agreement with the sheriff and then we'll get back to you."

While Clyde and Rusty refilled their glasses, Nicholas and Cole walked over to where the sheriff was talking to a group of men and took him aside.

"I've convinced Rusty and Clyde to make another go of it, Russell," Nicholas said. "So, do we have a deal?"

"Yeah, I guess so," Russell said, nodding his head. "Jared and Amos are happy about the chance to make some extra money and we were planning on riding back to Telluride tomorrow anyway. Besides, putting an end to these hold ups is part of our jobs."

"Good, I'll have the wagons ready to go at four in the morning," Nicholas said in a cheerful tone.

"Why so early?" Russell asked with a surprised look.

"Well Russell, I'm afraid I've always been a bit superstitious and when I find something that works, I hate to change it. Lady luck was smiling on us during our last trip. So, if you don't mind, Russell...I'd like to do everything the same way on this trip and maybe she'll smile on us again."

"Fine, I'll tell my men and we'll see you in the morning."

"No need to run off, Russell. Stay and have another drink."

"Thanks, but I need to stop in and visit with Marshal Bradley for a while before he leaves the office, so I better run along," Russell said.

After shaking hands with Nicholas and Cole, Russell and his two deputies thanked Misses Grant for the cake and then they left. A few minutes later, Nicholas called his workers together and announced his plans to send out another shipment on the following morning. Immediately after the announcement was made , the corks were replaced in the remaining bottles of whiskey and Grant's workers set about taking care of the mules and making preparations for the next day's shipment.

"Now then, lads, shall we go to my office and take care of getting you paid?"

Cole, Rusty, and Clyde followed Nicholas to his office where Nicholas offered them another drink, but only Clyde accepted.

"Now then, about your pay," Nicholas said after pouring himself and Clyde a drink.

"You can just transfer the money you owe me into my account at the bank," Cole said.

"How about you, lads?" Nicholas asked Clyde and Rusty.

"Well, it don't make sense to be walkin' around with all that money and risk losin' it," Rusty said. "So, I reckon if we could just get a little kick around cash, we could leave the rest in the bank, too."

"Don't forget we got's to pay Cole back the money he lent us," Clyde reminded Rusty.

"I can take the money you owe me out of your share of the four hundred," Cole suggested. "By the way Nick, you never did say how much you wanted for the cost of the replacement mule."

"Well...I've given that some thought and I've decided the three of you can keep the whole four hundred. I'll cover the cost of that mule out of me own pocket."

Cole suspected that his sister had a part in Nicholas's decision, but he joined Rusty and Clyde in expressing their appreciation for his generosity. Then after deducting the amount he was owed, Cole gave Clyde and Rusty the balance of their split of the four hundred dollars and Nicholas accompanied Clyde and Rusty to the bank. Once their accounts were established, Nicholas transferred the sum of $250 into each of their accounts and after shaking hands, Clyde and Rusty walked to the hotel with broad smiles stretched across the width of their weathered and stubble covered faces.

# Chapter Seven

When Russell walked into the Ridgeway Marshal's Office, Marshal Bradley was sitting at his desk reading last week's copy of The San Miguel Examiner which was printed in Telluride and the regions only newspaper.

"Afternoon Bradley," Russell said as he walked into the office.

"Hello Russ, I heard you were in town," Bradley said as he stood up and shook Russell's hand.

"Yeah, I just brought over a gold and silver shipment from Telluride."

"Any trouble?"

"No, no trouble."

"Sit down, take a load off," Bradley said. "You want some coffee?"

"No thanks, I just thought I would stop in and find out what's been going on around Ridgeway."

"Not much," Bradley replied. "We've had the usual trouble with drunks and such on the weekends and a few petty thefts. Matter of fact, Mike Fish is out arresting a fellow right now for stealing some chickens."

"I heard you had a couple of cowboys from Texas robbed at gunpoint a few days ago?" Russell said somewhat surprised by Bradley's failure to mention it.

"Where did you hear that?" Bradley asked trying not to show his surprise.

"Amos heard it from one of the victims."

"Yeah, I guess it slipped my mind because we got no leads and Fish was the one that took the report."

Both men turned their attention to the door as Bradley's deputy, Mike Fish, entered the office with Danny Brewer who had been seen stealing two of Misses Lyons's prize laying hens.

"What do you have to say for yourself, Dan?" Bradley asked the chicken thief.

"I'm sorry, Marshal. My mind was all messed up with the fever. I reckon it was the devil's work because when I woke up this morning, I felt something awful and the only thing I could think of to cure me was some chicken soup."

"Okay Mike, lock him up," Bradley said trying to keep a straight face. "We'll take him before the town council tomorrow and see what his punishment will be."

"Bradley, you ever hear of a lawman by the name of Todd Hanley?" Russell asked as Mike Fish led the chicken thief to one of the two cells.

"No can't say I have. Is he from Colorado?"

"I don't know, but he'll be buried in Colorado. He was one of the men that tried to hijack Nicholas Grant's last whiskey shipment. Nicholas hired him as a guard based on his claim that he was a former lawman."

"Well I'll be damned," Bradley said trying to look surprised. "I heard there was another attempted hijacking."

"Yeah, all the details will be in today's edition of the San Miguel Examiner."

"I figured as much. I should get a copy of the latest edition on this afternoon's stage," Bradley said. "Any leads on the other men involved?"

"Maybe...The other two men that were killed during the attempted holdup were both shot in the head. Unfortunately, there wasn't much left of their faces, so we have no idea what they look like. But, a man named Drew Williams was seen in Placerville, talking to Hanley and another man on the evening before the holdup attempt. We know Hanley is dead and based on Drew Williams' description of the man with Hanley, we think the man might be one of the other two that was killed during the holdup attempt," Russell explained.

"I know who Drew Williams is," Mike Fish said as he returned to the front office.

"How do you know Williams?" Russell asked.

"Well, I don't really know him like a friend or anything, but I've seen him around town several times and I've talked to him a few times," Mike Fish replied. "I'm sure you know him too, Jonas."

"No I don't think so," Bradley replied quickly.

"Sure you do, Jonas," Mike said in an unsuspecting tone. "Drew Williams and that fella he's usually in town with stay in that old run down cabin on the other side of town."

"Oh yes, I know who you're talking about now," Bradley said trying not to show his increasing concern. "But, I didn't know his name was Drew Williams. Don't think I've seen him around town for quite a while."

"Matter of fact, I just noticed lights in that cabin of theirs last night when I was making my rounds," Mike said still unaware that Jonas Bradley was lying.

"What does the fellow that is usually with Williams look like?" Russell asked.

"He's pretty ordinary looking, about medium height with shaggy brown hair and sometimes he's got a beard."

"Do you know his name?"

"I'm pretty sure his last name is Taylor. I can't remember his first name, but I know it starts with the letter B."

Neither Russell nor Mike Fish noticed that Bradley was becoming increasingly nervous as Russell asked, "How do you know his name starts with the letter B?"

"Because, he wears a fancy tooled holster rig with the initials B T stamped in it."

"Are you sure the letters weren't M T?" Russell asked after getting over his initial surprise.

"No, I remember admiring it pretty closely one time when he and Williams were hanging around over at the Galloping Goose Saloon and I'm positive the letters were B T," Mike said with a curious look.

"That's awful peculiar. One of the men killed during that last hijacking attempt was also wearing a fancy tooled holster rig, but the initials on it are M T and when I questioned Drew Williams yesterday in Placerville, the description Williams gave me of the man with Hanley matched that of the dead men who was wearing the fancy holster rig. Matter of fact, the description wasn't that different from the one you just gave for this fella, Taylor."

"Did Williams mention the holster rig and initials?" Mike asked.

"He mentioned the fancy holster, but I don't recall what he said about the initials," Russell said, his forehead wrinkled in thought. "I remember asking Williams about the initials, but I can't remember if he said the initials were MT or if he merely said there were initials on the rig. I guess it doesn't really matter because I've seen the dead man's holster and the initials are positively M T."

"Well then, I reckon the dead man ain't Taylor," Mike said. "I wonder if the same leather crafter made both holsters."

"It's possible," Russell replied. "Why don't we walk over to that cabin you mentioned and see if this fella, Taylor, is there? I'd like to take a look at his gun belt. If it is the same... maybe, whoever made the two holsters can tell us who the one with the initials MT belongs to. Either way... I'd like to ask Taylor a few questions."

"If you don't mind, I'll let you two go talk to this man, Taylor. I've got a letter I'd like to finish. So, I can get it on the morning stage."

"Okay Jonas, I'll catch you later," Russell replied.

Mike Fish and Russell left the jail and walked across town to the rundown cabin.

"Don't look like anyone is around," Mike said as he and Russell were approaching the cabin. "They usually keep their horses in that corral behind the cabin when they're in town."

"This place is a dump," Russell said once they were at the cabin.

"Yeah, it's seen better days, alright," Mike said grinning. "It sits empty most of the time except when Williams and Taylor are in town."

"According to Williams, he's in the business of buying and selling," Russell said. "Takes money to be in the buying and selling business. If Williams has any, you sure couldn't tell it by the looks of this place."

"Maybe, he just doesn't care about keeping it up."

"What do you say, we have a look inside," Russell said as he walked up onto the rickety porch.

"Whatever you say, Russ. I'm just a town deputy," Mike replied, chuckling.

Russell knocked loudly on the door which in itself practically forced the door open. After receiving no response, Russell pulled a large folding knife from his pocket and used the large blade to jimmy the door open.

"The inside is almost as bad as the outside," Russell chuckled as he stepped inside the one roomed cabin.

"Anything special, I should be looking for," Mike asked as Russell started looking in and under everything.

"No, let's just see if we can find anything that will tell us what Williams and Taylor have been up to," Russell replied as he pulled back the bedding on one of the two cots.

"Take a look at this!" Mike said after unfolding a wrinkled piece of brown paper that was on the floor.

"What is it?"

"It's got a bunch of cyphering on it," Mike replied as he put the paper on the table and flattened it out. Then after taking a closer look, he added, "Kinda looks like a breakdown of money into four splits."

"I think you're right," Russell said as he joined Mike at the table.

"Looks like they started with $580, but that's scratched out and changed to $380. Looks like someone named Sally got $38, Williams and Bart...that's it...Bart!" Mike said grinning. "Taylor's first name is Bart!"

"BT...Bart Taylor," Russell said smiling. "Makes sense."

"Yep, looks like Bart, Williams, and JB, whoever that is, each got $114."

"Any idea who Sally or JB could be?"

"The preacher's wife is named Sally and there's a gal that works at the Galloping Goose Saloon named Sally. As for JB... we obviously got

Jonas Bradley," Mike laughed. "But we also got Jerry Burke, Jim Brown, John Brewer, Justin Bull, Janet Baker and probably a hand full of others in town with those initials."

"Didn't you mention earlier that Bart Taylor and Drew Williams frequent the Galloping Goose Saloon?"

"Yeah and now that you mention it, those two Texans that were robbed a few days back...one of them said he was with Sally earlier that night and Jerry Burke is one of the bartenders at the Galloping Goose. I didn't really think Sally was involved, but just to be doin' my duty... I went over there to ask her some questions and I remember Taylor and Williams were in there playing cards at the time. And now that I think about it...those two Texans said they lost nearly three hundred dollars apiece!" Mike said with a surprised look on his face.

"So this $580 might be the actual amount Taylor and Williams took off of those Texans."

"Yeah, they probably scratched it out because they skimmed two hundred dollars off the top and then split the rest," Mike said still looking surprised. "And I bet JB is Jerry Burke!"

"Well, I'll let you and Jonas follow up on what happened here in town and talk to Sally and Burke. I'm guessing there's a lot more that Taylor and Williams are involved in," Russell said. "When I get back to Telluride I'll have Judge Tolbert issue arrest warrants for the two of them."

After Russell and Mike finished searching the cabin, which turned up nothing else of interest, Russell went to the hotel to inform his deputies of the latest discoveries and Mike Fish returned to the jail to inform Jonas Bradley.

"Jonas, you'll never believe what me and Russell found in that cabin," Mike said in an excited voice as he entered the office.

"What did you find?" Bradley asked as he quickly swept the envelope he had just sealed into his top drawer.

Beads of sweat started to appear on Bradley's forehead as Mike showed Bradley the piece of paper.

"Remember those two Texans that were robbed," Mike said in an excited voice. "Well, it looks like Sally, Drew Williams, and Bart Taylor were all involved."

"What about these initials? I wonder who JB is? " Bradley asked as he looked at the paper with a smile designed to hide his growing concern.

"I figure JB is Jerry Burke."

"That's pretty good detective work, Mike," Bradley said feeling somewhat relieved.

"You want me to go over to the saloon and bring Sally back here for questioning? I figured we would start with her."

"No, I'll do it. I need to take this letter over to the post office to make sure it goes out on the morning stage. You just wait here and we'll question her together."

As Bradley opened his desk drawer to retrieve the letter, he noticed a dirk in the drawer that he had taken off of a drunken prospector several weeks back. As he removed the letter, he also palmed the knife and slipped it into his vest pocket without Mike seeing it.

"I'll be right back, Mike," Bradley said as he left his desk and started for the door.

Jonas Bradley walked briskly toward the post office hoping that the pace would help calm his nerves.

"Hello Marshal," the postmaster said as Bradley entered the small clapboard building.

"Hello Harold, will you make sure this gets out on the morning stage?"

"Mister Drew Williams, care of the Placerville Palace Hotel," the postmaster read aloud, "Sure will, Marshal that'll be five cents."

Bradley handed the postmaster a nickel and then abruptly left. When he reached the Galloping Goose, Bradley quickly turned down the alley leading to the back of the saloon where there was an exterior stairway to the second floor. The stairway was designed as a fire escape, but it was frequently used by some of the prominent men in town who wanted to be discrete when visiting or leaving the second floor of the saloon. After quickly looking around to ensure no one was watching, Bradley dashed up the stairs and quietly made his way down the narrow hallway to the room at the end. Although it was still too early in the day for any of the girls to see much action, Bradley listened at the door for the sound of heavy breathing or any other noises that might indicate Sally was not alone. After hearing nothing, Bradley tried the door knob. When it turned freely, he quietly opened the door and peered inside. Sally was lying in her bed napping. Bradley stepped inside and gently closed the door behind him. Then he tiptoed to the side of her bed. Sally's eyes opened suddenly and a startled look appeared on her face, but before she could scream, Bradley shoved his hand over her mouth and pulled the knife from beneath his vest. He plunged it into her chest again and again until he felt her go limp. Then he slit her throat as an extra precaution before removing his hand from her mouth.

Sally's lifeless eyes continued staring at Bradley as he wiped the blood from his hands on the sheet. Then he did the same to the knife

71

before placing it back under his vest. After taking a moment to look himself over for any other traces of blood, he cursed, and a panicked look appeared on his face when he noticed several spots of blood on his sleeves and the front of his vest. His hands started to shake as Bradley tried to think of what to do. After a few minutes, he walked to the window and parted the thin, sun faded curtains just enough to see out. When he saw no one, Bradley raised the window and tossed the knife into the tall grass and bushes behind the saloon. Next he pulled back the covers and picked Sally up. Bradley's shirt sleeves and the front of his vest immediately turned red when they came in contact with Sally's blood soaked night gown. He carried Sally's body to the door and fumbled to open it, but his blood soaked hands kept slipping on the porcelain door knob. When he finally managed to get the door open, he raced down the hallway shouting, "Somebody get the doctor!"

As Bradley passed by the other rooms, Susie and Roberta, two of the saloon's other working girls, opened their doors and peered into the hallway to see what all of the noise was about. Roberta fainted almost as soon as she saw Sally's blood covered body, while Susie ran along behind Bradley shrieking, "What happened?"

"Somebody go for the doctor!" Bradley shouted again as he reached the first floor and laid Sally's body one of the tables.

One of the regulars at the bar ran for the doctor while the bartender and the other five men in the saloon rushed over to take a closer look at Sally.

"What happened?" Jerry Burke, the bartender, asked as he put an ear close to Sally's mouth.

"Looks like she's been stabbed," Bradley replied in a somewhat harried voice. "I went up to her room to ask her some questions and this is the way I found her."

"I don't think she's breathing," Jerry replied.

Bradley put his hand on Sally's chest as if he were actually checking for it to rise and then said, "I'm afraid she's dead."

"Why would anyone hurt, Sally," Susie asked, crying hysterically.

"She must have gotten into it with someone over the price of her services," Bradley said with a sad expression as he closed Sally's eye lids. Then turning to Jerry, he asked, "How about getting me something to cover her up with?"

"Susie, go upstairs and get a blanket," Jerry said as he put his arms around her shoulders and ushered her towards the stairs.

"Who was Sally's last customer, Jerry?" Bradley asked as the bartender returned to the table.

"I'm not sure she's had one yet today...at least not that I'm aware of. If she did, he must have gone up the back way."

The doctor arrived a few minutes later and a crowd began to gather outside the saloon as word of the stabbing started to spread through town. When Mike Fish noticed the crowd, he went to investigate as did Russell and his deputies who were in the café. After the doctor confirmed the obvious, Bradley had Jerry close the saloon and while they waited for the undertaker, Bradley repeated the story about finding Sally to Mike and Russell. After hearing the story, Mike and Russell went upstairs to look for clues while Bradley remained down stairs.

"Find anything worthwhile?" Bradley asked when Mike and Russell came back down stairs.

"No, afraid not," Russell replied. "Is that door to the back stairs always left unlocked?"

"From what I understand, it's left open for the convenience of certain visitors, if you get my drift," Bradley replied and then added quickly, "But, I assure you I'm not one of them."

"How come you carried Sally's body down stairs after you found it?" Russell asked with a puzzled look.

"I thought she was still alive and I was trying to get her some immediate help," Bradley replied.

"She sure did a number on your shirt and vest," Mike said.

"Yeah, I'm afraid they're ruined," Bradley said as he looked down at the front of his vest.

"How come you went up the back stairs to get her instead of coming through the front door?" Russell asked, but with no hint that he was suspicious.

Bradley glanced over at Jerry Burke who was mopping up the blood that had dripped onto the floor and then in a quiet voice said, "If Jerry is in on robbing those two Texans, I didn't want him to skip out before Mike and I had a chance to question him. So, I figured I would go up the back stairs and bring Sally down the same way."

Bradley took Russell's nod as a sign that he believed the explanation and a satisfied smile crept across his face.

The undertaker arrived and once Sally's body was removed, the saloon was reopened for business and while Bradley went home to change clothes, Russell and Mike stayed in the saloon to make sure Jerry Burke didn't try to leave. When the relief bartender arrived, ending Burke's shift, Mike and Russell escorted him to the jail for questioning. After three hours of intense questioning and not so much as a hick up from Jerry Burke that might indicate he had a part in the plot to rob

Rusty and Clyde, he was released and the identity of the man whose initials were on the piece of paper, found in the cabin, remained a mystery.

# Chapter Eight

Rusty and Clyde arrived at Grant's warehouse shortly before four o'clock in the morning. The wagons were loaded and the teams hitched up and ready to go. Russell and his deputies arrived a few minutes later after retrieving their horses from the livery.

"We just put a pot of coffee on and there's some of that cake left from yesterday. You're all welcome to some before we start out," Cole said after exchanging greetings with all the men.

The men helped themselves and once the coffee pot was empty, they shook hands with Nicholas and made ready to leave.

They were about half way to Placerville when the morning stage overtook them on its way to Telluride. The men exchanged waves with the stage driver and shotgun guard as it sped by. The mules had an inkling to give chase, but Rusty and Clyde quickly settled them down to their regular pace. It was midafternoon when the two wagons rolled into Placerville without any incidents along the way. Drew Williams was sitting in a chair on the boardwalk in front of the hotel. He sat up straight as he recognized Russell riding just ahead of the two wagons and when he spotted Cole on the lead wagon, he got up and moved into the open doorway to avoid being seen. Williams continued watching the wagons until they were well past the hotel and then he hurried up to his room. After grabbing his rifle and quickly stuffing some of his other belongings in his saddlebag, Williams left the hotel and hurried to the livery stable for his horse.

"Surprised to see you fellas back so soon," Mister Luze shouted as he walked out of his barn.

"We're a little surprised ourselves," Cole said as he hopped down from the wagon and shook Luze's hand.

"I see Nicholas finally sprung for a couple extra guards too," Luze said.

"Just for this trip, I'm afraid," Cole said as Russell and Jared dismounted. "This is Sheriff Douglas and this is his deputy, Jared Walters. The other fella with Rusty is Deputy Crabtree."

"Good to meet you," Luze said as he shook hands with Russell and Jared.

"Would it be alright for the sheriff and his deputies to keep their horses here for the night instead of taking them over to the livery stable?"

"I reckon so, but it'll cost Nicholas an extra buck."

"That's no problem," Cole replied.

"Alright, you know the routine. Go ahead and pull the wagons inside," Luze said as he started for the barn.

Once the wagons were inside the barn, Cole paid Luze the usual three dollars plus the additional dollar for the three horses. As soon as the horses were unsaddled and the mules free of their harnesses, the animals were put in the adjoining corral and the large double doors at both ends of the barn were closed.

"Myself, Rusty, and Clyde will bed down in here tonight, Russell," Cole said as he pulled his bedroll out of the wagon. "You and your men are welcome to bed down with us or you can get a room in the hotel."

"If it's all the same to you, Cole, I think I'll get a room at the hotel with one of my deputies. I'll leave it up to the odd man to decide if he wants to share a room with a stranger or bed down here with you fellas."

"Suite yourself, Russell, we'll take turns eating and staying with the wagons, but one of us will be here at all times."

"What time do you want to head out in the morning?" Russell asked.

"I'd like to be on the road at six," Cole replied.

"Okay, we'll be here to saddle our horses a few minutes before time to roll," Russell said with a casual wave.

***

It took Drew Williams just under four hours to reach the gang's hideout near Ophir. Bart Taylor, Pedro, and the two new Mexican recruits were sharing a bottle of whiskey and playing cards to pass the time while Brock Gilbert was standing watch a short distance down the road from the abandoned stamp mill that the gang used as their hideout. Brock cocked his rifle and ducked behind the boulder he was perched on when he spotted a rider leave the main road and continue toward the stamp mill.

"Howdy Drew," Brock shouted after recognizing Williams and rising up from his hiding place. "Didn't expect to see you so soon. Does this mean there's another shipment on the way?"

"Yep, two wagons just like the other day," Williams replied.

"Yahoo!" Brock yelled.

"I wouldn't be too quick to celebrate," Williams said. "We're up against those same three that was on the wagons last time. And this time they got the sheriff and his two deputies along."

"We still gonna try and take 'em?" Brock asked with a wide eyed expression.

"I don't know," Williams replied. "I'm not really sure we got any choice in the matter."

"Well, Pedro was able to find us two more men. They can't hardly speak a word of English, but they look plenty tough enough."

"Well, two more makes the odds a little better."

Williams left Brock at his post and rode on up to the hideout.

"Hello Drew," Bart Taylor said as Williams entered the hideout.

"Hey Amigo, good to see you so soon!" Pedro said with a broad smile. "I want you to meet our two new men. This is Juan and this is Roberto."

Williams quickly looked over the two men and agreed with Brock's assessment in addition to forming some additional opinions of his own.

After introducing the two men to Williams, Pedro said something in Spanish and toothless grins crept across both men's faces as they shook Williams' hand.

"I assume there must be another shipment on the way," Taylor said in an enthusiastic voice.

"Yeah, but I got good news and bad news. There's another shipment coming alright, but the same men that made the last run are on this one and the sheriff and his deputies are riding shotgun."

"Son of a bitch!" Taylor cursed as he hit the table with his fist. "Are we gonna try to take 'em?"

"We got to! We're already in hot water with Bradley and Joe Putra over the last shipment. We can't let another one get through!"

"Well, at least this time we don't have to worry about who we can and can't shoot."

"That reminds me...I found out what happened to Todd Hanley. He's dead."

"Who killed him?"

"I'm not sure, but somehow they figured out he was in on the last holdup attempt and they killed him."

"How did they figure that out?" Taylor asked with a shocked look.

"I don't know, but that's not all. Someone told the sheriff that they saw Hanley talking to me and you in Placerville on the night before the holdup and when I was in Placerville the sheriff and that fella, Cole Braxton...the one with the fancy rifle.... they came up to me and started asking me a bunch of questions."

"What kinda questions?" Taylor asked in a worried tone.

"Questions about you and Hanley, mostly."

"What did you tell them?"

"I told them that we just met and that I didn't really know either one of you. They asked me your name and when I told them I didn't know it, they had me describe you. But I think I tripped 'em up. I figured you and Mitch look enough alike that I gave 'em his description and when I finished...sure enough... they said the description sounded like one of the men that was killed in the holdup attempt."

"So, they thought it was my brother Mitch that was the one seen talking to Hanley?"

"Exactly," Williams said grinning. "Especially, after I described one of those fancy holster rigs you and your brother both wear."

"What if they figure out Mitch is my brother?"

"If they do, you can bet the sheriff is going to come looking for both of us," Williams replied. "So, you aughta think about getting rid of that holster rig of yours. It's too flashy for one thing. The last thing we need is to draw attention to us. Besides that, it will just make it easier for somebody to connect you and Mitch."

"I hate to just get rid of it," Taylor objected as he glanced down at his holster rig. "Me and Mitch gave fifteen dollars apiece to have these rigs made!"

"Too bad... that holster rig is a dead giveaway, now. So get rid of it," Drew Williams insisted. "Get yourself a plain rig like mine, instead of one that makes you stand out like a sore thumb."

"Well, I can't just stick me pistol in my pants like some sodbuster. But, I'll pick up a new rig after we pull off this next job."

"The sooner the better," Williams replied.

\*\*\*

The next morning, Russell and his deputies arrived at Mister Luze's barn just as Cole, Rusty and Clyde finished harnessing the mules to the wagons. The men talked and joked with each other as the horses were saddled, but there was a definite sense of tenseness among the men. Like the sheriff and Jordan, Amos was armed with a Winchester carbine in a 44-40 caliber. Although the 44-40 was a fine cartridge in its day, it lacked the range of the 45-75 caliber rifles that Cole, Rusty, and Clyde carried. As a result, after saddling his horse Amos tethered it to the back of the lead wagon and climbed up next to Clyde, while Cole joined Rusty on the second.

It was a few minutes after six when the wagons rolled out of Mister Luze's barn. The four mile jaunt to Sawpit along the San Miguel River took less than an hour and the sun was already banishing the heavy morning dew as the wagons started up the long grade toward Lizard Head Pass. When Russell and Jared pulled their Winchesters from their saddle scabbards, the men on the wagons checked their riffles and then Cole had Rusty slow his team to put a little distance between the two wagons. When they were about half way to the Telluride turnoff, Russell held up his hand as a signal to hold up. After resting the horses and mules as well as their own backsides for about half an hour, the men resumed their trek becoming more vigilant with each passing mile. Visions of their last experience flashed in and out of Cole's mind as they started across the long open stretch where the previous ambush had taken place. Although none of the men really believed that anyone would be so bold as to try another ambush in the exact same spot, they couldn't help expecting to hear gunshots at any second. When Clyde's wagon was about a hundred yards from the side of the outcropping where the mule had been shot, Russell and Jared suddenly put the spurs to their horses and galloped ahead. The plan was to have Russell and Jared ride ahead and check for horses that might be hidden in the trees at the far end of the open stretch, thus taking away the element of surprise if there were men hidden in the rock outcropping. The wagons continued at a steady pace with each passing minute seeming like an eternity once Russell and Jared disappeared into the trees. Clyde's wagon was within a few yards of where the mule had been dropped when Russell and Jared finally reappeared at the edge of the trees and gave the all clear signal.

When the wagons reached the cluster of trees, Clyde and Rusty pulled the teams to a stop and while the mules rested, the men took advantage of the opportunity to work some of the tension and stiffness out of their muscles and joints. After a thirty minute rest, the men were again on their way and when the Telluride turnoff came into view, each of the men felt a sense of relief. Then suddenly a volley of rifle shots rang out. Jared's horse went down as a bullet tore into its shoulder throwing Jared to the ground. At the same time one of Clyde's lead mules screamed as a bullet hit it in the neck. Clyde and Amos dove from the wagon as a second bullet hit the mule. The mule's knees buckled and it collapsed in a tangled heap. Rusty stopped his team and quickly wrapped the reins around the brake handle. A bullet grazed his left arm as he grabbed for his Winchester. Then an instant later the canteen hanging on the wagon seat by his side exploded, spraying water in all directions as Cole jumped from the wagon. It took the men just a few seconds to gather their wits, once they were off the wagons and Russell was off his horse. Then with the exception of Jared who had broken his collar bone and lost his rifle in the fall from his horse, one by one the men began returning fire as they spotted the telltale puffs of gun smoke on the hillside east of the road. Cole and the others had little difficulty determining where the shots were coming from, but the ambushers had taken time to gather rocks and build breastworks around three separate positions which even Cole's bullets could not defeat. So after a taking few shots, Cole quit firing and shouted to the others to save their ammunition.

"All we want is the whiskey!" Drew Williams shouted once both sides quite shooting. "Throw out your guns and you can walk away!"

"How do we know you won't shoot us anyway?" Russell yelled back.

"You have my word on it! All we want is the whiskey!" Williams replied.

"That's not very comforting coming from a bunch of dry gulchers!" Cole yelled.

"Try it one at a time if you don't believe me! You'll see I'm a man of my word!" Williams shouted.

There was dead silence for several minutes as both Cole and Russell considered their options and tried to come up with a plan.

"How bad is Jared?" Cole shouted just loud enough to be heard by Russell.

"He's not hit, but he's busted up pretty good," Russell replied.

"You got any ideas, Russell?"

"Not any good ones. How about you, Cole?"

"Maybe one," Cole replied. "If I could make it back down the road to those trees, I could use them as cover and try to work my way up to the top of the ridge and come at 'em from behind."

"Those trees are too far away. You'll never make it!" Russell replied after considering the plan. "They'll cut you down before you get half way there!"

"On foot maybe, but I was thinking of trying it on Amos's horse?"

Russell remained silent for a moment as he again considered Cole's plan and then replied, "Might work... providing you can get to Amos's horse."

"I'm willing to try it!" Cole replied.

"You want me to try to bring the horse to you?" Amos asked loudly.

"No, you and Clyde just help Russell and Rusty keep those bastards pinned down for a couple seconds."

"Okay, just say when!" Amos replied.

"On the count of three," Cole said as he got off the ground and crouched behind the front wagon wheel.

80

Cole counted to three and as he took off running toward the lead wagon, Rusty started firing his rifle and the others joined in. The move caught the men on the hill off guard and Cole was already half way to the lead wagon by the time they reacted. Pedro and the other two Mexicans fired off hurried shots, but the poorly aimed bullets fell well short of Cole as he dropped down behind the rear wheel of the lead wagon. The shooting ceased and Cole remained by the rear wheel panting heavily until he caught his breath. Then Cole stood up just enough to reach the reins on Amos's horse and pull it around to the protected side of the wagon.

"How about it, Sheriff?" Williams shouted. "Are you going to give up?"

"Give us a minute to talk it over!" Russell replied.

"Okay, but you better decide pretty quick!"

"Try to stall him and keep him talking," Cole shouted to Russell.

"Okay, good luck," Russell replied just loud enough for Cole to hear. Then cupping his hand around his mouth, he shouted, "Okay, we're gonna take you up on your offer!"

Cole rose up again and slid his rifle into the saddle scabbard as Williams shouted back, "Alright throw out your guns!"

"Okay, but we're gonna do it one at a time!" Russell replied as Cole moved around to the left side of the horse and tightened up the cinch.

"Alright boys be ready, here I go!" Cole said loudly as he put his foot in the stirrup and grabbed the saddle horn.

Amos and Clyde took aim at the ambusher's positions and as soon as Cole swung up into the saddle, they opened fire. Cole put the horse into a gallop and leaned forward in the saddle with his head next the horses neck. Rusty and Russell joined Amos and Cole pumping lead at the outlaws as fast as they could work the levers on their Winchesters. The ricocheting bullets and flying fragments of rocks did a good job of keeping the outlaws pinned down and the few shots they did manage to fire at Cole fell well behind him.

When Cole reached the cluster of trees, he jerked his rifle out of the saddle scabbard and pulled sharply on the horse's reins. The horse skidded to a stop and Cole dismounted on the run leaving the horse untethered.

"Hey Williams, what we do now?" Pedro shouted to Williams once Cole was out of sight.

"We still got plenty of time," Williams replied. "It'll take that rider a couple of hours to reach Sawpit for help. It'll be dark by then and we'll be long gone by the time any help can get back here."

81

From Williams' reply it was obvious that he thought the rider who had escaped was going for help when in reality, Cole was already making his way up to the top of the ridge. After hearing Williams' reply, Pedro repeated the message in Spanish to the two Mexicans that were by his side.

"Hey Sheriff, I bet you think that was pretty clever sending a man for help!" Williams shouted. "There's just one problem...by the time help arrives it'll be too late! Once it gets dark we'll be on top of you and you'll all be dead! And for what...a bunch of whiskey! You got one minute to throw out all your guns and walk away!"

Williams pulled out his pocket watch and watched the seconds tick by. When the minute was up, he shouted to Pedro, "Kill all the mules on the first wagon and fill the wagon with lead!"

"You mean shoot up the whiskey?" Pedro asked in a surprised voice.

"That's right. Time to show these bastards we mean business and if we can't take the whiskey, at least we can keep it from getting to Telluride!"

Pedro translated Williams' instructions to his two comrades and the men replied with evil grins. The three Mexicans laughed and howled as they slaughtered the helpless mules where they stood and then they started pumping lead into the bed of the wagon. In a matter of seconds, whiskey began seeping between the gaps in the wooden wagon floor and before long both Amos and Clyde were drenched in the stuff.

"By god... killin' those poor mules was one thing...wastin' good whiskey is another!" Clyde muttered in an angry voice after catching a few drops of whiskey on his tongue. "Them sons of bitches better hope I never meet up with them."

The shooting stopped and restarted several times as Pedro and his fellow Mexicans emptied their guns and then reloaded. Then suddenly a more distant and much different shot echoed across the valley. Cole's first bullet caught Pedro square in the back as he was casually reloading his rifle. The two Mexicans at his side spun around instantly and looked toward the top of the ridge. A second shot rang out and a split second later the Mexican on the right of Pedro was violently thrown back against the rocks as a bullet shattered his sternum. The surviving Mexican threw down his rifle and raised his hands as he screamed, "Tener compasión! No disparar!"

The man's voice was quickly drowned out by another gunshot and he crumpled over backwards as a bullet tore through his heart and lung. Cole racked another round into the chamber of his rifle and quickly took aim at Brock Gilbert's revetment which was about fifteen feet to the south. Gilbert was doing his best to become invisible, but both legs were fully exposed. Cole took a deep breath and fired. Gilbert cried out in agony as a bullet shattered his right femur severing the artery. Then seconds later he lost consciousness as a second bullet shattered the bone in his other leg. Without so much as a brief pause, Cole automatically worked the lever on his rifle and swung it further south to the position shared by Williams and Taylor, but by then both men had managed to crawl away and conceal themselves in a small crevice between some nearby boulders. After continuing to scan the rocks for several minutes, Cole stood up and waved at the men by the wagons. The men spotted Cole immediately, but it took a while before they realized that he was trying to signal them to continue toward Telluride. Amos and Clyde cautiously crawled out from under the wagon and hurried up the road to where Russell and Jared were nestled down in the ditch while Rusty kept his rifle trained on the slope.

After helping Jared back to the second wagon, the men rearranged several of the whiskey cases and once Jared was lifted into the bed of the wagon, Amos and Rusty climbed in behind him, while Russell and Clyde scrambled up on the driver's seat. Clyde started the team, but as the wagon approached the disabled one and the mules started to smell their dead comrades, they refused to continue until Rusty and Amos climbed out of the wagon, blindfolded the lead mules with their bandannas, and began pulling on their bits. It took quite an effort, but with Amos and Rusty pulling and Clyde lashing at their backsides, they finally managed to coax the mules around the first wagon. By the time Amos and Rusty pulled the blindfolds and clambered back into the back of the wagon, they were both exhausted, but their spirits were high. Minutes later the men exchanged final waves with Cole and as the wagon disappeared around a bend in the road, Cole sank back down in the rocks to continue watching for the remaining ambushers.

They came across Russell's horse grazing by the side of the road at the Telluride turn off. Clyde stopped the wagon just long enough for Russell to catch and mount his horse and then they continued. When the men reached Telluride, Clyde drove the wagon to the doctor's office so that Jared could get his broken collar bone taken care of and it took some persuading, but they finally managed to talk Rusty into having the doctor take a look at his grazed arm as well. After agreeing to meet at the Yellow Canary Saloon, Russell remained with Jared and Rusty while Clyde and Amos took the wagon to Nicholas Grant's warehouse.

"Well, I'll be damned!" Charlie Duckfoot said when he spotted the wagon coming. "Who'd a thunk it? Two shipments in one week!" Then turning to his helpers he shouted, "Get them doors open! We got another shipment rollin' in!"

"Howdy, Charlie!" Clyde shouted after pulling the team to a stop.

"Hello, yourself!" Charlie replied in an excited voice. "Never expected to see you back here. I figured you'd be half way to the Pecos by now!"

"Well, me and Rusty decided to make another go of it," Clyde said grinning as he climbed down from the wagon and shook Charlie's hand.

"How'd you get talked into riding shotgun, Amos?" Charlie asked as he shook hands with Amos. "You give up bein' a deputy?"

"No... me, and Russell, and Jared were coming back anyway. So, we decided we might as well make a little side money and ride along with the whiskey wagons."

"You run into any trouble?"

"Yeah, afraid so," Clyde replied. "Bushwhackers hit us right before the turnoff."

"Anybody get hurt?" Charlie asked with a concerned expression.

"Jared busted up his shoulder when his horse got shot out from under him, but the doc says it'll mend and Rusty got shot in the arm," Clyde replied. "But the bullet just nicked him, so it ain't bad. In fact, I've seen him horse bit worse. "

"What about the other wagon?"

"They shot it up and killed all the mules, so we had to abandon it."

"What about the bushwhackers? Did they get away?"

"Don't know for sure," Amos said. "Cole managed to sneak up behind 'em and we heard five shots, but we pulled out without talking to him," Amos said.

"Well, if I know Cole...five shots probably means he got five of 'em," Charlie said with a big grin. "Where's Cole now?"

"Last we saw of him... he was still up on that ridge," Clyde replied in a seemingly unconcerned voice.

"You mean you left him out there alone?" Charlie asked with a surprised expression.

"Had to... Besides, that's what Cole wanted. After we heard them five shots, he motioned us to be on our way. But, I imagine Cole will be a long after a while," Clyde said in a confident voice.

\*\*\*

Cole remained on top of the ridge hoping that the remaining ambushers would show themselves, but once the sun started to set, he decided to leave the ridge by the same way he had come before it was too dark to navigate the steep and rocky terrain. He found Amos's horse not far from where he had dismounted and caught it with little trouble, but he knew that trying to ride back up the road would be too risky. So, he waited until it was totally dark before mounting the horse and continuing toward Telluride.

Taylor and Williams also waited until after it was totally dark before making any attempt to leave their hiding place. Although the night sky was clear and full of stars, the absence of a moon made it extremely difficult and slow going for Taylor and Williams as they made their way back to where they had hidden the horses. It was well into the evening by the time they reached their horses and both men were bruised and battered. They drank from their canteens as they sat on the ground discussing what to do next. Then after several minutes, they untied all the horses and led them through the thick timber down to the road. Once they reached the road, Taylor and Williams mounted their horses and with the horses belonging to the dead men in tow, they continued toward the Telluride turn off.. When they reached the turnoff, Williams turned toward Telluride and Taylor continued toward the hideout with all of the extra horses.

# Chapter Nine

On the morning following the second hijacking attempt, Cole, Rusty, and Clyde rode out to the ambush sight with a team of four mules to recover the wagon and see if there was anything left of its contents that could be salvaged. As a favor to Russell, they also agreed to recover the bodies of the dead outlaws.

Across town, Drew Williams was just leaving the house of a female friend where he frequently stayed when he was in Telluride. He walked to the warehouse owned by Joe Putra which was only a few blocks from the one owned by Nicholas Grant. Williams used a side entrance to enter the building and walked down a short hallway that led to Putra's private office. Williams could tell by the look on Putra's face that he was already aware that a portion of another whiskey shipment had reached Telluride. Once the door to Putra's office was closed, Putra unleashed his anger. Although Putra was an educated man from a wealthy eastern family, he was not a well-spoken man and often had difficulty expressing himself even when he was calm. And when he was angry, his sermons generally became rambling tirades full of illogical threats. Although Williams was tempted to grab Putra by the throat and put an end to his abusive behavior, Williams didn't have the backbone to stand up to him, so he remained calm and said little until Putra finished delivering his tongue lashing.

"I'm sorry, Joe," Williams said once Putra started to wind down. "I did my best to stop the shipment. I even lost four men trying, but those fellas Grant hired are just too good. And to make things worse... the sheriff and his deputies were riding with them!"

"Then get better men! That's what I pay you for!" Putra shouted.

"I've been trying, but it's not like I can just run an ad in the newspaper like you do when you need help," Williams said starting to lose his temper.

"I don't care! It's bad enough that you haven't been able to steal Grant's whiskey, forcing me to actually bring in my own stuff, but when you can't even prevent Grant's shipments from getting here...you force me to lower my prices or lose customers. Damn it, Drew...you're putting me out of business!"

"At least we stopped one of the wagons from making it," Williams replied in a defensive tone.

"That's not good enough! I need you to make sure Grant's warehouse stays empty!"

A sly grin suddenly appeared on Putra's face as he thought of a new scheme.

"There's more than one way to skin a cat," Putra laughed. "I want Grant's warehouse destroyed! I want you to burn it down!"

"Burning down Grant's warehouse might result in burning down half the town!" Williams said with an astonished look.

"I don't care, I want it destroyed! You can burn it down or blow it up with dynamite! I just want it gone!"

"A lot of innocent people are liable to get killed," Williams replied in a matter of fact voice.

"Since when do you give a damn about killing innocent people?"

"I was just stating a fact," Williams replied, shrugging his shoulders. "When do you want it done?"

"As soon as possible. Tonight for all I care. The more whiskey that gets destroyed in the process the better!"

"How about tomorrow night? It's a Sunday and folks generally turn in early on Sunday. The town aughta be pretty quiet by midnight or so."

"Fine Sunday it is!" Putra replied with an evil smile.

***

When Cole, Clyde, and Rusty reached the ambush sight, it was obvious that a number of wild animals had been at the mule carcasses throughout the night, but only a bunch of fat crows and magpies were still present. After securing the mules and horses a short distance from the wagon, the men walked to the wagon on foot and used the axes that they had brought with them to hack the carcasses into manageable pieces, while being careful not to damage the harnesses. Once all of the carcasses had been thrown over the side of the steep incline on the west side of the road, the men started inspecting the contents of the wagon. Only a few of the bottles were unbroken, but for the most part the bullets that hit the whiskey barrels had only pierced the upper half leaving most of them still half full. After throwing the damaged bottles and the few unsalvageable kegs over the embankment, Cole led Rusty and Clyde up to the rock revetments where he had shot the four bandits. It took quite an effort and considerable time to carry all four bodies back down to the wagon. As a result, it was late in the afternoon by the time the replacement team was hitched to the wagon and the men started back to Telluride.

***

After leaving Putra's office, Williams got his horse and rode to the hideout near Ophir.

"What did Putra have to say?" Bart Taylor asked as Williams entered the stamp mill.

"About what you would expect," Williams laughed. "He ranted and raved for a few minutes. I was tempted to snap the little weasel's neck, but I stood there and let him spew it all out. And he came up with a new plan...He wants us to burn down Grant's warehouse tomorrow night."

"Be a hell of a fire!" Taylor said. "Be lucky if it doesn't burn the whole town down!"

"Putra doesn't care! All he cares about is himself and putting Nicholas Grant out of business."

"So, we gonna do it?'

"Yeah, I figure late tomorrow night we'll ride into Telluride and get the job done."

"What about the night watchman? Grant ain't dumb enough to leave the place unguarded."

"It's probably just some old coot with a shotgun and he'll likely be asleep by the time we get there," Williams chuckled. "It won't matter anyway because I don't intend to break in. I noticed a couple gallons of coal oil in that old tool shed out back. I figure we'd take a couple tins of that along with us and just dump it on the outside of the warehouse. Once that old wood siding gets started, the whole place will be ablaze in no time."

***

When Cole, Rusty, and Clyde arrived back in Telluride they stopped the wagon in front of the Sheriff's Office and Cole went inside. Cole and Russell emerged a few minutes later and Rusty threw back the bullet riddled canvas so that Russell could take a look at the four bodies.

"Never seen those two before," Russell said pointing at the two Mexicans. "These two look somewhat familiar which means I've probably seen them around town a few times, but I don't know their names or anything about them."

"Any chance you might have seen their likenesses on a wanted poster?" Cole asked.

"I doubt it, but I'll go through my stack of old posters just to be on the safe side. Anyway, I sure appreciate you bringing them in. Things will be pretty tight for me until Jared is able to come back to work."

"Glad to return a favor," Cole said.

"Well, if you wouldn't mind doing me another, I'd appreciate it if you would drop the bodies off at the undertakers. Tell him, I'll be over later to sign the papers."

"No problem, we're on our way to Grant's warehouse and it's on the way."

"You fellas gonna be in town awhile?"

"Just till Monday," Cole replied. "Figured we'd head back to Ridgeway with at least one of the wagons first thing Monday morning. Now that a shot of whiskey is back down to two bits, we'll probably be at the Yellow Canary after we drop of this wagon at the warehouse. If you care to stop by later, I'll buy you a drink...or two," Cole said smiling.

"I appreciate the offer, but with Jared out of action Amos and I are putting in some long days. I've got to be back by midnight to relieve him, so I'm gonna go on home and catch some shut eye."

"Alright Russell, I'll see you next time we're back in town," Cole said as he shook Russell's hand.

Clyde and Rusty also shook hands with Russell and then after throwing the tattered canvas back over the bodies, they continued on to the funeral home.

*** 

Shortly before midnight on Sunday night, Russell left his modest home on Pine Street and started walking toward the jail. When he reached Pacific Street a noise that sounded like rattling cans caught his attention and he noticed two men on horseback with gallon cans strapped to their saddle horns. Russell moved into the shadows and continued watching the men as they rode past and then he started to follow them. The two men turned down Willow Street and continued toward the river until they were directly in front of Grant's warehouse where they stopped. Russell closed in, hoping to hear what the men were saying and as the men dismounted, he pulled his gun and stepped out of the shadows.

"Hold it right there. What are you men up to?" Russell asked.

There was a silent pause as both Taylor and Williams recognized the sheriff's voice. Then Williams whispered to Bart, "You answer him, Bart. If I do it, he'll recognize my voice."

"We ain't up to nothing," Taylor said loudly. Then pretending that he was unaware, he asked, "Who are you anyway?"

"I'm Sheriff Douglas. Now what are you men doing out here in the middle of the night?"

"We were just on our way down to the river, Sheriff," Taylor replied in a crackling voice.

"What have you got in those tins?"

There was another brief silence as Taylor scrambled to come up with a reasonable answer and then he replied, "They got whiskey in 'em Sheriff, and to be honest ...we were gonna water it down a little before we tried to sell it up at the mines."

"Whiskey?" Russell repeated in a surprised and doubting voice. "Since when does whiskey come in gallon tins?"

"Truth is, it didn't exactly come from no regular whiskey peddler, Sheriff," Taylor said in an almost apologetic and remorseful tone. "We bought it off of some prospector."

"Where did the prospector say he got it?"

"Said he come across a shot up whiskey wagon up on the road to Lizard Head Pass. But he managed to save a little and he put it in these here tins."

Not only was Taylor's explanation possible, it was also logical and Russell actually believed it. So as he started walking closer to inspect the tins, he holstered his gun and when he did, Drew Williams pulled his gun and fired. Russell was hit, but before going down, he managed to pull his own pistol and shoot back, hitting Taylor in the leg and spooking the horses. Williams cursed as he walked closer to Russell and put two more bullets into Russell before realizing that Taylor had been shot.

"Help me up," Taylor said in a pain filled voice as he tried to stand.

"You won't make it far on foot with a bullet in your leg," Williams replied.

"You can't just leave me," Taylor said.

"You're right," Williams said as he cocked his pistol and quickly placed it to Taylor's head.

As the last gunshot echoed through town, a few lights appeared in the dark houses further up the street and before long some of the inhabitants spilled out into the streets to find out what all the shooting was about. The night watchman in Grant's warehouse was at the very back of the warehouse when the shots first rang out and by the time he reached the front entrance everything was quiet. After cautiously unlocking the front door, he proceeded outside with a shotgun in one hand and a lantern in his other. A few minutes later, the watchman spotted the bodies lying in the middle of Willow Street and his cries for help quickly summoned a number of other residents to his location.

90

Later that morning, Joe Putra woke at his regular time and got out of bed with a smile on his face. He leisurely followed his usual morning routine and then he walked to the Smuggler Café where he had breakfast every morning. When Joe Putra walked into the café, it was buzzing with conversations. Putra paused by the door with a big smile, eaves dropping on the conversation. But his smile quickly faded when he realized that the conversations were about a shooting with no mention of any fire.

"Morning, Mister Putra," Belle, the waitress, said as Putra sat down at the counter.

"What's this about some shootings?" Putra asked.

"Sheriff Douglas got in a shootout with some stranger last night and they killed each other!" Belle replied as she automatically filled a coffee cup and sat it in front of him.

"Where did that happen?" Putra asked with a genuinely surprised look.

"Over on Willow Street," Belle replied.

"Willow Street," Putra repeated, looking even more surprised. "I heard there was also a fire over there last night."

"No... Thank God...there was just the shooting."

"Are you sure?"

"Yes...I'm sure," Belle replied with a puzzled look. "If there was a fire in town, I'm sure I would have heard about it."

"Yeah, I guess you're right," Putra said trying not to show his building anger.

"Are you ready to order, or would you like a minute to look over the menu?" Belle asked, smiling.

"I think I'll just have some coffee," Putra replied after looking at his pocket watch. "I need to catch the morning stage."

"Going on a trip?"

"Just a short one," Putra replied. "I just have some business in Ridgeway."

While Putra was in the Café gulping down his cup, Cole, Rusty, and Clyde were just getting ready to check out of the hotel when the desk clerk informed them of the shootings. After getting over the initial shock, the three of them were full of questions, but the clerk was only able to repeat what he had heard.

"Sorry fellas, all I know is that Sherriff Douglas shot it out with some man and they both ended up killing each other."

"Any idea who the other man was?" Cole asked.

"No, apparently he was a stranger in town," the clerk replied.

"Where did it happen?" Clyde asked.

"Over on Willow Street.'

"Ain't that the street where Nicholas Grant's warehouse is?" Clyde asked.

"Matter of fact, the shooting happened right out in front of the warehouse," the clerk replied. "Jim Fuller, the night watchman, was the one that found the bodies after he heard the shooting."

"I guess we won't be checking out after all," Cole told the clerk.

"Should I hold your rooms for another night then?"

"I'm not sure," Cole replied as he started for the door.

"No problem, Mister Braxton," the clerk replied. "Just let me know. Check out time isn't until ten o'clock, anyway."

"Where we goin', Cole?" Rusty asked once they were outside.

"I thought we would walk over to the sheriff's office," Cole replied. "Maybe Amos can answer some of our questions."

"Good idea," Rusty said, nodding. "Don't it seem awful strange that the shootings took place in front of Nicholas's warehouse?"

"Maybe, Russell lives near the warehouse," Clyde suggested.

"Could be," Cole admitted. "But, it still seems mighty coincidental."

"You think the shootings have something to do with the whiskey shipments?" Clyde asked.

"I don't know, but the fact that the shootout occurred right in front of the warehouse...it sure seems like there must be a connection," Cole replied. "And if there is...I'm hoping Amos might be able to give us some information that will help us put the pieces together."

When they reached the sheriff's office, they were all surprised to see Jared in the office instead of Amos.

"Figured you would be home in bed," Cole said as he shook Jared's left hand.

"I came in as soon as Amos sent me word about Russell," Jared replied as he shook hands with Clyde and Rusty.

"We just heard about Russell. I sure am sorry. We didn't know Russell for very long, but we all thought he was a hell of a man," Cole said. "If there's anything we can do to help you and Amos out...all you gotta do... is let us know."

"Thanks Cole, I will," Jared replied. "Amos just left a few minutes ago to go home and catch a little sleep. We're gonna meet with the county commissioners this afternoon to figure things out."

"The hotel clerk didn't seem to have much information," Cole said, nodding. "So, we were hoping maybe you or Amos could fill in some of the missing pieces."

"I'll try, Cole. Me and Amos are still trying to figure things out ourselves, but I'll be glad to share what information we do have."

"Thanks, I'd appreciate it," Cole said. "At this point all we heard was that Russell shot it out with another man in front of Nicholas Grant's warehouse and they both killed each other."

"Well, that's what we thought originally, but once the undertaker had a chance to look over both the bodies and we started gathering the facts…that's not at all what happened!" Jared said. "Matter of fact, the dead man never even fired his gun."

"So, there had to be at least one other man involved!" Cole said with a surprised look.

"That's right and it doesn't look like it was Russell that actually killed the other man either."

"How do you know that?" Rusty asked.

"Because, the other man was shot twice...once in the leg and once in the head, but Russell's gun was only fired once," Jared explained. "And...Russell was shot three times, once from a distance and twice at close range, but the dead man's gun was still in his holster and it was unfired."

"So whoever killed Russell... also killed the other man," Rusty said with an even more surprised look.

"Any idea who the other man is?" Cole asked.

"We got a pretty good idea it's Bart Taylor," Jared said as he pulled a holster rig from the bottom desk drawer. "Remember this holster?"

"Yeah, it's the one we took off that dead outlaw after the first attempted hijacking," Cole replied after glancing at the holster.

"Take a closer look," Jared said as he walked to a cabinet across the room and opened it.

"The initials are different!" Cole said with a surprised expression after looking at the holster.

"That's right. We got that holster this morning off of the dead man that was found with Russell. The initials are BT which we figure is for Bart Taylor," Jared replied as he pulled a second holster rig from the cabinet and then handed it to Cole. "This is the holster we took off of that hijacker you killed."

"BT and MT…same last initials," Cole said as he compared the two holsters and then passed them to Rusty.

"Except for the initials... they look exactly the same," Rusty said as he handed the holsters to Clyde.

"Exactly! So, me and Amos figure Bart Taylor and that outlaw we took the other holster off of were probably brothers!"

"I'll bet you're right," Cole agreed. "Which probably means Bart Taylor was also in on the whiskey hijacking operation."

"Yeah, and we figure since Bart Taylor and Drew Williams were working together in Ridgeway, he's probably in on the whiskey hijackings as well."

"If that's the case...I wonder if Williams was the third man involved in last night's shootout?"

"Me and Amos were wondering the same thing," Jared replied. "The way me and Amos got it figured...Russell probably saw Williams and Taylor hanging around Grant's warehouse and when he confronted them, they went for their guns. At some point, Williams must have shot Russell and Russell must have shot Taylor in the leg. Then after Williams finished Russell off, we figure he killed Taylor."

"Man would have to be lower than a snake's belly to kill his own partner!" Clyde said.

"If Taylor was shot in the leg, Williams probably figured Taylor would slow him down too much," Rusty said.

"And Williams couldn't just leave Taylor behind because he was afraid Taylor might talk," Cole added.

"Yeah, that's the way me and Amos had it figured, too," Jared said.

"Sounds like we need to find Williams!" Cole said with an angry expression.

"You reckon he's still around town?" Rusty asked.

"Hard to say, but with both Russell and Taylor dead...and no other witnesses...Williams has got no reason to think we're on to him," Jared replied.

"Yes, but we also know Williams hangs around Placerville and Ridgeway, too. So, he might be headed for one of those places until things get settled here in Telluride," Cole said.

"That's true... fortunately, Marshal Bradley is already on the lookout for Williams in Ridgeway as a suspect in robbing Rusty and Clyde," Jared said.

"Have you sent a telegram to Marshal Bradley about Russell?" Cole asked.

"Not yet, I haven't had a chance. But, I will and I'll let him know that Williams is a suspect in Russell's killing, too."

"Well, before we heard about Russell, the three of us were planning to head back to Ridgeway," Cole said. "We could give you and Amos a hand looking for Williams round Telluride for a while and then we could head for Ridgeway like we planned. We can spend the night in Placerville and take a look around town for Williams while we're there."

94

"I'm sure me and Amos can handle things here in Telluride, but if you fellas would take care of looking for Williams in Placerville, that would be a big help," Jared said with an appreciative smile.

"Like I said... we'd be glad to help anyway we can," Cole replied.

"Well, if you fellas are gonna help out...it might be a good idea to deputize the three of you, so it's all official and you can legally arrest Williams if you do find him."

"Any objections?" Cole asked Rusty and Clyde.

"No, I guess not," Rusty replied.

"Me neither," Clyde replied.

"To be honest, I'm not sure I got the authority to do this, but I doubt anyone will be opposed to it, anyway...so, raise your right hands."

Jared swore Cole, Clyde, and Rusty in as San Miguel County Deputy Sheriffs and then handed them each a deputy badge.

"Been on a posse or two before, but I never had no badge of any kind before," Clyde said, grinning as he took the badge.

"Me neither," Rusty said, with an even bigger grin.

"Well, I figure there's no reason to show our hand or let people know we're deputies unless we need to. So, it would probably be best if we all keep these badges hidden," Cole said as he placed his badge inside his shirt pocket. "Besides that, they make good targets."

"Well, now that you mention it...I sure don't need no target pinned to my shirt," Clyde said laughing.

# Chapter Ten

The morning stage, with Joe Putra onboard, was just pulling away from the Telluride depot as Cole, Clyde, and Rusty were leaving the sheriff's office. The three of them stopped by the hotel and after checking out, they walked to Grant's warehouse.

"You fellas decide to sleep in? We had the wagon all hitched up and waiting for you over an hour ago!' Charlie Duckfoot said as Cole and the others entered the warehouse.

"Sorry Charlie, we were over at the sheriff's office talking to Jared Walters," Cole replied.

"I guess you know about Russell Douglas being killed then," Charlie said with a sad expression. "Happened right out front there. In fact, it was my night watchman, Jim Fuller, that found the bodies."

"Yeah, so we heard," Clyde said as he tossed his gear into the back of the wagon and climbed in after it.

"Ain't you gonna drive," Rusty asked as he climbed up into the wagon seat.

"No, I'll let you take 'em," Clyde replied grinning. "I figured you could use more 'sperience handling a team and I could try to catch up on some sleep. So, try not to jostle me around too much!"

"If you would have turned in when me and Cole did, instead staying up half the night drinkin' and ridin' whores, you wouldn't need to catch up on your sleep!"

"Maybe so, but I figure one of us aughta try living up to the reputation of a Texas Cowboy!" Clyde replied as he lay down in the back of the wagon and pulled his hat down over his eyes.

"They ever figure out who that man was?" Charlie asked as Cole was just about to climb up next to Rusty.

Cole looked around and then in a low voice said, "Yeah, we think so, but we want to keep his identity a secret for the time being."

"What for?" Charlie asked with a confused look.

"Because we think that man was one of the whiskey hijackers and we don't want to scare off the others before we can catch 'em. So, don't say nothing to nobody."

"I'll be damned! I been wonderin' if there was a reason the shootout happened right here in front of the warehouse," Charlie said with a surprised look. "You think that fella was gonna try breaking into the warehouse?"

"I'm sure he was up to something," Cole replied. "You're watchman hear any voices or have any idea what led up to the shooting?"

"No, he said he was clear in the back of the warehouse when he heard the shots. By the time he got to the front of the building the shooting was all over and he never did see nobody. Then after a few minutes, he went outside to take a look around and that's when he spotted the two bodies out there in the middle of the street."

"Well, might be smart to double your guard at night, anyway."

"Yeah, I'll do that. You fellas still gonna stay on for at least one more shipment?"

"Yeah, I imagine we'll be back in a few days with another load," Cole replied.

"By the way, when you see Nicholas, tell him Mister Ritter said it'll be sometime next week before he'll be able to bring those replacement mules up here from Cortez."

"Okay, I'll tell him."

"Alright, take care, fellas!"

"See you, Charlie," Rusty said as he started the team.

When they reached Placerville, Rusty drove the wagon to Mister Luze's barn and once the team was unhitched the men walked to the Placerville Palace Hotel.

"Afternoon gents, what can I do for you?" the hotel clerk asked.

"We'd like a couple of rooms," Cole replied.

"You fellas look familiar, so I assume you've stayed here before and you know that we require two men to every room."

"Yeah, we're aware of the rule," Cole replied. "Put these two gentlemen in one room and I'll take my chances in another."

"Alright, just sign the register," the clerk said as he reached for three room keys.

After signing the register, Cole ran his finger down the two facing pages looking for Drew Williams' name.

"I see Drew Williams is registered," Cole said when he found the name. "Is he still here?"

"You fellas friends of Williams?"

"More like acquaintances you might say," Cole replied.

"We're still holding his room, but he must have gotten tied up somewhere on business because I haven't seen him for a couple of days. Matter of fact we been holding a letter for him since last Thursday."

"Any chance you could put me up in his room," Cole asked as he laid an extra dollar on the counter. "I know he has an arrangement for a

97

private room and I would sure rather share a room with an acquaintance than a total stranger."

"Well, I don't know about that," the clerk said.

"I doubt Williams will mind and if he does, you can always move me to another room," Cole said as he put another dollar on the counter.

"Yeah, I guess I could do that," the clerk said as he looked around and then swept the two dollars off the counter.

"I appreciate that," Cole said with a friendly smile.

"Williams' room is number 10," the clerk said as he exchanged keys.

Clyde and Rusty followed Cole upstairs and after pausing briefly to drop their gear in room 5, they continued down the hall to room 10. Cole knocked on the door just to make sure no one was inside and then he unlocked the door.

"Why don't you two go back downstairs and keep an eye out for Williams while I go through his things," Cole said.

"What should we do if we spot him?" Rusty asked.

"Arrest him," Cole said chuckling. "Or just shoot him if you have to."

"Wouldn't that save us all a lot of trouble?" Clyde laughed as he and Rusty started back down the narrow hallway.

Most of the rooms in the hotel were almost identical with basic furnishing which typically consisted of two chairs, two metal framed cots, a small chest of drawers, a small wardrobe, and a single nightstand with a kerosene lamp. After looking under the beds, Cole stripped off the bedding on both beds, but he found nothing. He then searched the wardrobe and chest of drawers which turned up a combination of clean and dirty shirts, dungarees, socks, and underwear which Cole piled on one of the beds. After emptying the chest of drawers and wardrobe, Cole went through all the garment pockets which resulted in nothing but some loose change, a few matches, and some cigarette rolling paper. Cole had already decided that the search of Williams' room was going to be a waste of time when he noticed the single drawer on the nightstand. Cole opened the drawer and after seeing that it contained nothing but a blank piece of slightly wrinkled paper, he again closed it. Cole was just about to leave the room when he paused at the door and then returned to the nightstand. He pulled the paper out of the drawer and held it up to light streaming through the single window. Then he folded the paper, placed it in his pocket, and left the room.

\*\*\*

When Joe Putra arrived in Ridgeway on the afternoon stage, he went directly to the marshal's office. Jonas Bradley and his deputy, Mike Fish, were in the office talking about the death of Sheriff Douglas when Putra stormed into the office.

"Uhhh Hello Joe," Bradley said with a surprised expression.

"I'd like to have a word with you, Jonas...in private," Putra said trying not to show his anger, but doing a poor job of it.

"Sure thing, Joe. Have you met my deputy, Mike Fish?" Bradley asked in a nervous voice.

"No, I don't believe so," Joe Putra said trying to act cordial.

"Mike, this is Joe Putra, he's a business man from Telluride."

"Nice to meet you, Mister Putra," Mike said extending his hand. "What brings you to Ridgeway?"

"Just a quick business trip," Joe Putra replied trying to force a smile.

"Mike, how about taking a turn around town and give me some time to talk to Joe alone," Bradley said trying to act normal.

"Okay sure... Nice to have met you, Mister Putra," Mike said as he grabbed his hat from the coat rack by the door and left the office.

"What the hell is going on, Jonas?" Putra shouted in an angry voice.

Bradley motioned for Putra to keep his voice down as he quickly moved across the office and closed the door leading to the cell area.

"I know you're mad, Joe. But I got a prisoner back in the cells, so try to keep your voice down."

"Damn it Jonas, are you trying to ruin me? What kind of men have you got working for you? Your idiots have let two shipments through! It's bad enough that I'm out the whiskey and have to haul in more of my own, but now I'm also losing business! And that idiot Williams that works for you, he can't even handle a simple job like burning down a damned warehouse!"

"Burning down a warehouse?" Bradley asked with a confused look.

"Yeah, Grant's warehouse, you fool!"

"I don't know anything about that," Bradley said still looking confused.

"Since your men can't seem to stop Grant's shipments from getting through, I told that bungling idiot, Williams, to burn down Grant's warehouse in Telluride. But what does he do? He ends up getting his partner shot and killing the county sheriff! It's one thing to kill a few no account freight wagon drivers and steal some whiskey, but killing a county sheriff...we'll be lucky if the governor doesn't declare Martial Law and send in the National Guard!"

"I can't help that, Joe. Burning down Grant's warehouse wasn't my idea. You should never have told Williams to do it," Bradley said in a defensive voice.

"Who the hell do you think you are telling me what I should or shouldn't do?" Joe Putra screamed. "Are you forgetting who pays who?"

"No, but I knew things were getting too hot. I sent Williams a letter last week telling him to lay low for a while after the sheriff found out that he and Taylor robbed those two Texans and now because of what happened last night, I got a telegram from one of the sheriff's deputies informing me that Williams is a suspect in the sheriff's murder and they also know he and Taylor were in on the whiskey hijackings."

"What Texans? What robbery?"

"The same two Texans that have been driving Grant's wagons for the past week. The sheriff was going to get arrest warrants issued for Williams and Taylor."

"Why wasn't I informed about any of this? You know how I hate surprises!" Joe Putra said in a voice that indicated his anger was building again. "If I had known the were wanted, I would never have told them to burn down Grant's warehouse."

"Like I said, this all just happened last week. What did you expect me to do, send you a telegram and risk linking Taylor and Williams to us?"

"Don't get smart with me, Jonas! You should have told Williams and Taylor to get out of Colorado immediately!"

"I'm tired of hearing what I should have done, Joe!"

"I don't give a damned what you're tired of. You're still on my payroll!" Putra shouted.

"Not any more, Joe. I'm through! This scheme of yours is getting way too hot and without Williams and Taylor, I'd have to start over and recruit a whole new outfit! And if you're smart you'll lay low too."

"What do you expect me to do...rollover and just let Grant put me out of business?" Joe Putra asked with fire in his eyes.

"I don't know. Why don't you talk to Grant? Try to work out a deal with him or offer to buy him out."

"That's not a bad idea!" Joe Putra said with a sly grin. "But I might need you to lean on him a little."

"I can't do that. Nicholas Grant is a well-liked man here in Ridgeway. He's friends with the mayor and everyone else on the town council. Like I said, I'm through with this whole thing!"

"I'll decide when you're through!" Joe Putra said in an angry voice as he turned and left.

When Joe Putra left the office he was fuming with anger, but by the time he reached Nicholas Grant's office and warehouse, he had regained his business like composure.

"What can I do for you?" the guard asked as Putra stepped into the confined entry area.

"I'd like to see Nicholas Grant," Joe Putra said in a firm, business like tone.

"Could I have your name, sir?"

"Yes, I'm Joe Putra."

"I'll tell him you're here, Mister Putra."

A moment later Nicholas accompanied the guard to the front of the office saying, "Sorry about all this security, Mister Putra, but I'm sure you've heard about all the trouble I've been having."

Once the guard unlocked the door to the confinement area, Nicholas extending his hand to Putra and said, "It's a pleasure to finally meet you, Mister Putra."

"It's a pleasure meeting you too," Putra replied as he shook Nicholas's hand with a limp grip.

"Come on back to my office, I got just the thing if you're thirsty," Nicholas said in a jovial tone.

Joe Putra followed Nicholas to his office and once they were inside, Nicholas said, "Sit down, Mister Putra. Make yourself comfortable.

"Mind if I close this door?" Putra asked.

"Not at all," Nicholas replied, shrugging his shoulders. "Now what can I get you to drink? How about some fine Scotch Whiskey?"

"No thanks, I'd like to get right down to the purpose of my visit."

"By all means, Mister Putra. I'm a man who appreciates a direct approach," Nicholas said as he poured himself a drink and then settled down in the chair behind his desk.

"I'd like to make a deal with you, Mister Grant."

"Ohhh...what kind of a deal?" Nicholas asked with a broad smile.

"I'd like for you and I to come to an agreement on the prices we're going to charge for whiskey."

"An agreement on prices!" Nicholas said with a surprised expression.

"That's right... I want you to stop selling your whiskey so cheap. We can both make a lot more money if you'll just raise your prices to a reasonable level. You're just throwing away profit. If we work together, we can charge whatever we want for our whiskey. The saloon owners and the chumps that drink our whiskey will pay whatever they have to."

101

"Well now, Mister Putra, I'm certainly not opposed to making more money," Nicholas said after taking a drink of Scotch. "But, I think my prices are high enough now."

"A few weeks ago, I was getting five hundred dollars a barrel for whiskey in Telluride and the saloons were getting a buck a shot! If the miners and the other working stiffs want a drink, they'll figure out how to get the money for it!"

"Aye maybe so, but I'd rather make more money by selling more whiskey at a reasonable price than simply by raising me prices and gouging honest working men out of their hard earned wages."

"I'm not saying we have to stick with my prices, but there's no sense continuing to bump heads. We can meet someplace in the middle and we can both get rich."

"I wasn't aware we were bumping heads, Mister Putra," Nicholas said after taking another drink. "I was under the impression that when your wagons get through, your business is good and when my wagons get through, my business is good. There's nothing wrong with a little competition to keep prices fair for everybody."

"I can't afford to charge less money for my whiskey, Grant. My expenses are twice what yours are and my losses are just as bad as yours."

"Aye, but from what I hear my lads have delivered some pretty good punches to them bastards that have been attacking our wagons. If they get their noses bloodied one or two more times, we may not have any more losses."

"Yes but, I still have to haul my whiskey all the way from Cortez."

"Maybe, you should think about giving up on Telluride and settle for the towns on the other side of Lizard Head Pass."

"I bet you'd like that, alright!" Putra said with an angry look. "But I don't need you to tell me how to run my business. You know I can't afford to give up Telluride. That would mean cutting my business in half."

"I'm not trying to tell you how to run your business, Mister Putra," Nicholas said becoming slightly defensive. "That's for you to decide."

"Alright Grant, if you're not interested in making a deal, how much will you take for your business? I'll pay you top dollar."

"My business isn't for sale, Mister Putra."

"Nonsense, everything is for sale! Just name your price!"

"Like I said, Mister Putra...my business isn't for sale," Nicholas said, starting to become slightly irritated.

"Don't be so sure. Things happen," Putra said with an angry look as he picked up a picture of Clair that was on Nicholas's desk. "Is this your wife?"

"Aye."

"Maybe you should think more about what's best for your wife," Putra said with a crooked grin. "Be a shame if something happened to her."

"My wife!" Nicholas said in an angry tone as he jumped to his feet, quickly walked around his desk, and grabbed Joe Putra by the front of his coat. "You think you can come in here and force me to sell out by threatening to hurt my wife?"

"I wasn't trying to threaten anybody," Putra said in a frightened tone as his beady eyes grew to the size of silver dollars.

"Get out of here you son of a bitch!" Nicholas shouted as he jerked Putra out of his chair with one hand.

Joe Putra's arms and legs flailed like a scarecrow in a stiff wind as Nicholas dragged him down the hallway toward the front door.

"Open the damned door, Chet," Nicholas shouted at the guard.

The stunned guard rushed to the door, quickly unlocked it, and jumped aside as Nicholas dragged Putra into the entry area and then tossed him out into the street.

"If that son of a bitch comes back, shoot him!" Nicholas said to the guard as he straightened his vest. "Imagine the nerve of that bastard, thinking he could come in here and threaten me."

After picking himself up out of the dirt, Joe Putra hurried back to the marshal's office and demanded that Bradley arrest Nicholas for assault, but Bradley refused. After listening to Joe Putra's angry tirade and threats for a few minutes, Bradley finally managed to calm Putra down.

"Go check into the hotel, Joe," Bradley said. "We'll get together in the morning and figure out what to do next."

"I want that bastard killed!" Putra insisted.

"We'll talk about in the morning," Bradley said as he ushered Joe toward the door.

\*\*\*

After killing the sheriff and Bart Taylor earlier that morning, Drew Williams made an attempt to catch his horse, but when he saw the night watchman's lantern, he ran to the river and hid in the thick willows along the bank. He remained hidden by the river for several hours until the bodies were taken away by the undertaker and the crowd of onlookers started drifting back to their homes. Once Willow Street was again dark and quiet, Drew Williams followed the river to the west end of town where he stole a horse and took off galloping toward Placerville. When he reached Placerville, Williams considered stopping at the hotel for a few hours rest, but he decided to push on toward Ridgeway.

It was late in the afternoon when he finally arrived in Ridgeway and both he and his stolen horse were about done in. Williams headed directly to the Marshal's Office and after hastily tying his horse to the hitching rail he rushed into the office.

Deputy Mike Fish was in the back cell area playing checkers with Dan Brewer, the chicken thief. Mike stood and walked to the front of the office as soon as he heard the door open and close.

"Where's Marshal Bradley?" Williams asked in a harried voice.

"It's his wife's birthday, so he went home a little early," Mike replied in a casual manner.

"Okay, thanks," Williams said as he turned to leave.

"Hold it right there and put your hands up!" Mike said as he pulled his pistol. "You're under arrest!"

"For what?" Williams asked.

"Just do as I say and put your hands up!" Mike said as he moved closer to take Williams' gun.

"What's this all about?"

"You're under arrest for robbery and suspicion of murder!" Mike said as he lifted Williams' pistol from his holster.

After prodding Williams back to the cell area at gun point and locking him in the cell next to Dan Brewer, Mike Fish hurried over to Marshal Bradley's house.

"Happy Birthday, Cathie," Mike said as Bradley's wife opened the door.

"Thank you, Mike," Cathie said smiling. "Won't you come in?"

"I'm kinda in a hurry to get back to the jail, so could you just tell Jonas I need to see him real quick?"

"Surely, I'll go get him," Cathie replied.

"What is it, Mike," Bradley asked in a slightly irritated tone.

"Sorry to bother you, Jonas," Mike said in an apologetic voice, but with a big grin. "I just figured you would want to know right away that I just arrested Drew Williams."

"Drew Williams!" Bradley repeated with a shocked look. "How? Where?"

"He showed up at the jail asking for you and I arrested him," Mike said still grinning.

"Okay, let me grab my hat and gun belt and I'll be right with you," Bradley stammered in a nervous voice.

"There's no real need for you to come back to the office, Jonas. I got him all locked up and everything. I just figured you would want to know."

"Well, I want to ask him a few questions, anyway... and I need to send a telegram off to Telluride to let the sheriff's deputies know we have him in custody," Bradley replied in a nervous voice.

After telling his wife that he needed to leave for a while, Bradley strapped on his gun belt, grabbed his hat, and then accompanied Mike Fish back to the jail. Drew Williams was sitting on the bunk in his cell with a panicked look on his face as Mike Fish and Jonas Bradley walked into the cell area.

"There he is," Mike said with a satisfied smile.

"Good work, Mike," Bradley said as he pulled his pistol and clubbed Mike over the head.

"What the hell you do that for?" Dan Brewer asked with a shocked look on his face as Mike Fish dropped to the floor.

"Shut up or you'll get the same!" Bradley threatened. Then turning to Williams he asked in an angry voice, "What the hell are you doing in Ridgeway? Didn't you get my letter?"

"What letter?" Williams asked with a surprised look.

"I sent you a letter last week telling you that the sheriff was on to you for robbing those two Texans!"

"How did he figure that out? Did that bitch, Sally talk?" Williams' asked in a surprised voice.

"We don't have time to go into that now; robbing those Texan's is the least of our worries. I got a telegram this morning from one of the deputy sheriffs. They know you killed Sheriff Douglas and Bart Taylor!"

"I had no choice!" Williams explained with a worried look. "Putra ordered me to burn down Grant's warehouse and that damned sheriff showed up when we were getting ready to torch the place. So, I had to shoot the sheriff and when Taylor got wounded, I had to kill him too."

"Yeah well, now they've tied you and Bart Taylor to the whiskey thefts."

"If that's the case, I better get the hell out of Colorado!"

"I'm afraid it's too late for that," Bradley said as he bent down and pulled Mike Fish's pistol out of his holster.

"What do you mean it's too late? Open this damned door!" Williams demanded.

Bradley shot Mike Fish with his own gun and then quickly shot Dan Brewer before pulling his own pistol and turning it on Williams.

"What the hell are you doing, Jonas? I thought we were friends!" Williams said with a panicked look as Bradley cocked his pistol.

"Sorry Drew, I'm afraid it's time to dissolve our friendship," Bradley said coldly.

"Why you double crossing son of a ..."

Bradley pulled the trigger before Williams could finish cursing at him and after shooting him a second time to ensure he was dead, Bradley quickly opened the cell door leaving the key in the lock and put Mike Fish's pistol in Williams' hand.

After hearing the shots, several men that were across the street from the jail rushed to the marshal's office and cautiously opened the front door with their guns drawn.

"What's going on in there?" one of the men yelled as he cautiously entered the office.

"Get the doctor!" Bradley shouted.

"Is that you, Marshal?"

"Yeah, get the doctor! Mike Fish has been shot!" Bradley replied.

One of the men ran for the doctor while the rest of the men hurried inside and crowded into the hallway leading to the cells.

"What happened?" one of the men asked as he kneeled down to check on Mike Fish.

"Better check on Dan Brewer, too! Looks like he's also been shot," Bradley said as he pulled the key from the cell door and handed it to one of the other men.

"Are you okay, Marshal," another man asked.

"Yeah, I'm fine."

"I'm afraid a doctor won't be able to help Mike now. He's dead!" the man that was checking on Mike Fish said.

"So is Brewer," the man checking on Dan Brewer said.

"What happened, Marshal?"

"I'm not sure," Bradley replied as he pried Fish's pistol out of Williams' hand. "I was on my way out the door when I heard a couple of shots from back here. I ran back here to the cells and when I saw Williams with this gun in his hand, I shot him."

"I've seen this fella, Williams, around town a few times. What did you have him locked up for?"

"Well, in case you haven't heard...Sheriff Douglas was killed last night and Williams is the suspected killer!" Bradley replied. "And he's also a suspect in those whiskey hijackings over by Telluride."

"I'll be damned!" the man replied.

"No wonder he was trying to escape!" one of the other men added.

"Judging from this gash on the back of Mike's head...Williams must have grabbed Mike from behind and bashed his head against the bars," the man kneeling by Mike's body said.

"Yeah, and then Williams must have grabbed the keys and Mike's gun," Bradley agreed, nodding his head.

"Wonder why he shot Brewer?" the man asked who had checked on Dan Brewer.

"Looks like, Mike's gun was fired twice," Bradley said as he rotated the cylinder and ejected two spent cartridges.

"Maybe, Mike's gun went off and Brewer was hit when Williams was trying to wrestle it away from him," one of the men speculated.

"Yeah, or Williams might have just shot Dan Brewer out of pure meanness," Bradley said.

"Well, at least the bastard got what was coming to him!" one of the men said and several of the others agreed.

When the doctor arrived a few minutes later, Bradley had everyone wait outside until the doctor was finished examining the bodies to confirm the obvious. Then he had several of the men carry the bodies outside and place them in the wagon that the undertaker had borrowed and once the undertaker left with the bodies, the crowd started to dissipate with most of the men drifting over to the Galloping Goose Saloon. Bradley spent a few minutes soaking up compliments from the mayor and a few of the other prominent citizens. Then he locked up the office and walked back to his home where his wife's birthday party was still in progress.

# Chapter Eleven

After searching Williams' room, Cole joined Clyde and Rusty who were watching for Williams while they sat on a bench in front of the hotel.

"Find anything interesting!" Rusty asked when Cole walked out of the hotel.

"Not really, just this piece of paper. It might be something or it might not," Cole said as he pulled the paper from his pocket and handed it to Rusty.

"It's blank," Rusty said with a puzzled look.

"Yeah, but hold it up to the light. You know how when you use a sharp pencil to write something on a piece of paper and there's another piece of paper under it... sometimes it kind of makes an impression on the second piece of paper. Well, if you look closely you can almost make out some names and numbers."

"Yeah, I see what you mean," Rusty said after holding up the paper. "But I can't make out what it says."

"Neither can I, but I read one of those dime detective novels once when I was in Chicago. I remember there was a detective that was faced with a similar situation. He rubbed his hand on the inside of a wood stove to get soot on his fingers and then he gently rubbed the soot on the paper so he could see what it said."

"You think it really works?" Clyde asked.

"I don't know, but I figure it's worth a try," Cole replied.

"There's that big potbellied stove in the bar," Clyde said, grinning. "We could get a drink and use some of the soot off that stove to try it."

"Okay let's do it," Cole agreed.

The men walked into the bar and ordered three whiskeys. Once the bartender poured their drinks, Cole paid for them and they walked to a table near the potbellied stove that was located in the middle of the room. After retrieving the paper from his pocket, Cole unfolded it and laid it out flat on the table. Then he opened the large door on the stove and ran his fingers across the inside until they were covered in soot.

"What do you know...it does work," Cole said as he lightly rubbed his black fingers across the paper.

"Can you read what it says?" Rusty asked in an anxious voice as he got up and leaned over Cole's shoulder.

"Looks like it says, Putra, Bradley, then the initials M E, and then Taylor," Cole said with a surprised expression.

"Could those initials just be the word... me?" Rusty asked.

"Of course... how stupid," Cole chuckled. "Fine detective I am. This is probably Williams' handwriting and he used the word...me... to refer to himself."

"Putra...ain't that the name of that whiskey peddler the bartender in the Yellow Canary mentioned?" Clyde asked.

"Sure is," Cole replied.

"What about the name Bradley? You think that could be Marshal Bradley?" Rusty asked with a wide eyed expression.

"I don't know, but I'm guessing these dates are the dates of the two whiskey shipments that were hijacked before we signed on and if they are, these numbers by Putra's name probably represent how much he paid for the stolen whiskey and these other numbers show how Bradley, Williams, and Taylor split the money they got from Putra."

"I reckon that explains what was happening to the stolen whiskey," Rusty said.

"You really think Marshal Bradley could be involved?" Clyde asked.

"Wouldn't be the first time a lawman went bad," Cole replied. "Remember Todd Hanley?"

"I wonder if Hanley and Bradley were friends?" Clyde asked.

"Well, if Marshal Bradley is involved, I'm sure they at least knew each other," Rusty said.

"Remember, when we checked into the hotel? The clerk said he was holding a letter for Williams," Cole said with a sly grin. "I think it's time we had a look at that letter."

Cole dabbed the end of his neckerchief in his whiskey and then used it to clean the soot off of his fingers. Then after downing the rest of his whiskey, Cole, Clyde, and Rusty walked to the hotel lobby.

"I'd like to take a look at that letter you said you were holding for Drew Williams," Cole said to the desk clerk.

"I can't give you that letter," the clerk said with a surprised look.

"Sure you can," Cole replied as he pulled the badge from his shirt pocket. "We're deputy sheriffs."

"But...but...I'm still not sure I can give it to you," the clerk stammered. "Don't you need some kind of a court order, or search warrant, or something?"

"Rusty, arrest him for interfering with the law!" Cole said in an official sounding voice.

Rusty shot Cole a surprised look and then trying to act official, he grabbed the clerk by the arm saying, "You heard Deputy Braxton...you're under arrest."

"Take him away, Deputy Gibb," Cole said.

"Wait a minute...wait a minute," the clerk pleaded. "I'll give you the letter."

Rusty looked at Cole and when Cole nodded, Rusty released the clerk's arm. The clerk turned around and pulled an envelope from a slot marked with a number ten and handed it to Cole.

"What's your name?" Cole asked the clerk.

"Bill...Bill Smith," the clerk replied in a nervous voice.

"Smith...huh? You wanted for anything, Smith?" Cole asked with a stern look.

"No sir!"

"Okay, we're still going to be around for a while. So, I want you to keep quiet about this. We don't want anyone to know we're deputy sheriffs," Cole said as he put his badge back in his shirt pocket. "You tell anyone and we'll arrest you. Is that clear?"

"Yes sir. I won't mention it to a soul!"

"Alright, thanks for your cooperation," Cole said before turning to leave.

Clyde and Rusty followed Cole and once they were outside, they all had a good laugh before taking a seat on the bench.

There's no return address, but according to the stamp it was sent four days ago from Ridgeway," Cole said as he inspected the envelope.

"You sure it's legal for us to open other people's mail," Clyde asked as Cole started tearing open the envelope.

"To be honest...I have no idea!" Cole said, looking at Clyde and grinning.

"What are you worried about, Clyde?" Rusty asked, laughing. "You think Williams is gonna bring charges against us?"

"No, I reckon not," Clyde replied, grinning.

"What does it say, Cole?" Rusty asked after Cole unfolded the letter.

"It starts out with Drew, but no last name," Cole said before starting to read the letter aloud. "Sheriff Douglas and Mike Fish searched the log cabin today and they found a piece of paper showing how we split the money you got off those two Texas cowboys. As a result, they know you, Bart, and Sally were involved. They don't know I'm involved, so I'll take care of Sally to make sure it stays that way."

"So, whoever wrote this letter killed that gal, Sally!" Clyde said interrupting Cole.

"Let him finish," Rusty barked with an irritated look.

"Sheriff Douglas is getting an arrest warrant for you and Bart," Cole continued. "So, stay away from Ridgeway. It looks like Grant is planning

110

to send out another shipment soon, but it might be better to lay low for a while even if Joe Putra doesn't like it...."

"There's Putra's name again!" Clyde repeated interrupting Cole again.

"Let him finish!" Rusty snapped giving Clyde another annoyed look.

"That's it," Cole said. "The last line just says for Williams and Taylor to remain at the hideout until he sends further instructions."

"Who is it signed by?" Rusty asked.

"It's not signed," Cole replied handing the letter to Rusty.

"So, Marshal Bradley is involved!" Clyde said with a surprised look. "And it was him that killed Sally, too!"

"It sure sounds that way," Cole agreed. "In fact it looks like Bradley is the boss of the whole outfit."

"You gotta admit, it's a pretty slick operation," Rusty said. "Taylor and Williams hijack the shipments, sell it to Putra, and Putra sells it just like it was his own whiskey."

"Now all we got to do is prove it!" Cole said.

"What do you reckon we aughta do next, Cole?" Rusty asked.

"First thing we need to do is let Amos and Jared in on all of this."

"We could send them a telegram tomorrow afternoon once we get to Ridgeway," Rusty suggested.

"Yeah, but I'd hate to have the telegraph operator leak out word of all this and have Marshal Bradley find out," Cole replied wrinkling his forehead in thought.

"If we waited to leave town until after the post office opens in the morning, we could send them a letter," Clyde said. "It would go out on tomorrow's stage and get to Telluride late tomorrow afternoon."

"Yeah, which means it would be delivered on Wednesday. Which means Jared or Amos could catch the stage on Thursday and be in Ridgeway on the same afternoon," Cole said. Then after considering it for a moment, he said, "Or I could borrow a horse from Mister Luze and ride back to Telluride myself first thing in the morning while you two take the wagon on back to Ridgeway. That way I could catch the stage with Amos or Jared Wednesday morning and be in Ridgeway a day sooner."

"Weren't they planning to bury Russell on Wednesday?"

"Yeah, I forgot about that," Cole replied. "I feel bad about not staying around for the funeral, but I thought it was best for us to get here and see if we could find Williams before he moved on. Anyway, I guess that means Amos and Jared wouldn't be able to leave Telluride until

Thursday morning. So, I guess we might as well just send them a letter on tomorrow's stage."

"You think there's a possibility that Williams might still show up here in Placerville?" Clyde asked.

"Hard to say," Cole replied. "He obviously never saw this letter. So, Williams still doesn't know he's wanted for his part in robbing you two and he doesn't know we're onto him for murdering Russell, either. So, I doubt he's actually on the run."

"Well, he's still got a room here in the hotel. So, maybe we'll get lucky," Rusty said.

"Maybe so. Anyway, I figured we'll hang out here and keep watching for him. Once it gets late, I'll sleep in his room just in case he does show up after we turn in."

The following morning, the three men ate breakfast together in the dining hall and after checking out of the hotel, they went to Mister Luze's barn. Once the mules were hitched to the wagon, Clyde drove it to the post office and after Cole mailed the letter he wrote to Amos and Jared, they continued to Ridgeway.

***

Earlier that same morning, Joe Putra met with Jonas Bradley in his office. What started out as a heated discussion, resulted in Putra losing control and shouting nonsensical threats at Bradley. The argument finally ended when Bradley promised to either kill Nicholas Grant himself or have the job done. Bradley had no intention of actually keeping his promise, but it was the only way he could think of to end the argument and get rid of Putra. Putra left the marshal's office shortly thereafter and after checking out of the hotel, he caught the morning stage back to Telluride.

That afternoon, Nicholas Grant was in his office when one of his workers informed him that Cole, Clyde, and Rusty had just returned from Telluride.

"Welcome back, lads!" Nicholas said in a loud jovial voice as he walked into the warehouse to greet them.

After shaking their hands and giving each of them a hearty slap on the back, Nicholas invited them to his office for a celebratory drink.

"Sounds like you had another bit of excitement," Nicholas said as he poured them each a drink of his best Scotch. "Well, thank god you all made it unharmed."

"I suppose you heard about Russell Douglas," Cole said.

"Aye, it's a terrible loss!" Nicholas said as he handed out the drinks. "We had some excitement ourselves here in town, you know."

"What kind of excitement?"

"The marshal killed that fellow, Williams!" Nicholas said. Then raising his glass he said, "Well here's to your health, gentlemen!"

"Bradley killed Williams?" Cole asked with a stunned look.

"Aye," Nicholas replied after taking a gulp of his Scotch. "Williams tried to break out of jail and the marshal shot him, but not before Williams killed that poor deputy and some poor lad that was locked up for stealing chickens."

"If Williams was locked up, where did he get a gun?" Rusty asked.

"Apparently, he grabbed the deputy's gun."

"Sounds like that deputy must have been awful careless!" Clyde said with a doubting look.

"Sounds pretty suspicious to me," Cole said. "Were there any witnesses?"

"Just the marshal," Nicholas said with a puzzled look. "What makes you think it seems suspicious?"

"Take a look at this," Cole said as he took the folded paper from his pocket and handed it to Nicholas. "I found this in Williams' hotel room in Placerville."

"I see the names Putra, Bradley, and Taylor, but what is it?"

"I'm guessing it was written by Williams, so the word 'me' stands for him. See those dates? Are those the dates of your last two hijackings?"

"By God...yes they are!' Nicholas replied with a shocked look.

"I thought so," Cole replied with a satisfied smile. "I'm guessing the amounts written by Putra's name indicate how much he paid for the stolen whiskey and the amounts by the other names, shows how the money was split up."

"But, how can that be? Some of Putra's wagons were also hijacked!"

"Were they really or were the hijackings just made up to keep everyone from becoming suspicious?" Cole asked.

"So that bastard, Joe Putra has been the one stealing my whiskey and murdering my drivers all along!" Nicholas said with fire in his eyes as he poured himself another Scotch.

"I'm not sure if he's the one behind it all, but it sure looks like he's the one buying your whiskey once it's stolen. The way I figure it, Bradley is the boss. Williams and Taylor take their orders from Bradley and do all the dirty work along with their gang of outlaws."

113

"Then why would Marshal Bradley kill Williams?" Nicholas asked after emptying his glass.

"For the same reason Williams killed Taylor...to keep him from talking," Cole replied.

"I thought it was the sheriff that killed Taylor!" Nicholas said with a surprised look.

"No, we're pretty sure that it was Williams that killed both Russell and Taylor," Cole replied.

"Now you've got me all confused!" Nicholas said as he refilled his glass.

"I got one more thing I want you to see," Cole said as he pulled the folded envelope containing the letter from his pocket and handed it to Nicholas."

"You think this was written by Bradley?" Nicholas asked after reading the letter.

"I'd bet every cent that you've paid on it!" Cole replied.

"If that's true then it was Bradley that killed that Sally woman in the saloon!"

"That's right!"

"Aye, if that's the case we should go to the mayor. He can help us organize a citizens committee to lock up that bastard, Bradley, until we can send for some real lawmen."

"That won't be necessary," Cole said as he pulled the badge from his other shirt pocket.

"What's this? You're a deputy sheriff now?"

"All three of us are, but we don't want anyone to know," Cole said somewhat amused by the look on Nicholas's face. "I already sent a letter to Amos Crabtree and Jared Walters."

"Aren't those the deputies that were with Russell Douglas last week?"

"That's right," Cole replied. "I'm sure one of them will be here on the Thursday afternoon stage. So, we plan on waiting until then before we do anything with Bradley."

"Can we afford to wait until then? What if that bastard, Bradley, decides to take off?"

"I don't think we have to worry about that. Bradley has no idea we're onto him and with both Williams and Taylor dead, he probably figures he's got nothing to worry about. But I'd like to put off any more whiskey shipments for a few days, so the three of us can kind of keep an eye on Bradley and be here when Amos or Jared get here."

"Aye, that's fine with me, but what about that other bastard, Joe Putra?" Nicholas asked still fuming with anger.

"I'm sure Amos and Jared will arrest him as soon as they get my letter," Cole replied.

"Aye, good work lads! Have another drink, you deserve it!" Nicholas said as he poured himself another Scotch and then offered the bottle to the others.

After finishing their drinks, Cole had Nicholas lock the letter and piece of paper in his safe. Then Rusty and Clyde walked to the hotel and Cole walked to Nicholas's house where he had been staying in the guest room.

The next morning, Cole met Rusty and Clyde at the café for breakfast.

"How close you reckon we need to watch Bradley?" Rusty asked Cole after Rita took their order and walked away.

"I figure we best give him lots of slack," Cole replied. "No reason to crowd him and risk tipping him off. Nicholas told me that Mike Fish's funeral is this afternoon. Wouldn't look right if Bradley was to miss it. So, I'm sure he'll be there and after the funeral, Bradley will probably go on home. So, all we really have to do is keep a casual eye on him from tomorrow morning until the stage gets here Thursday afternoon."

"You reckon it'll be Amos or Jared that comes here from Telluride?" Clyde asked after taking a gulp of coffee.

"Probably be Amos," Rusty said. "Wouldn't make sense for Jared to come what with his collarbone busted and his arm in a sling."

"I know, but Jared has got more 'sperience and he's the senior deputy, so I figure he'll be the one to come," Clyde replied. "What do you think, Cole?"

"I'm not sure," Cole replied. "Doesn't really matter to me which one comes. I figure the three of us will be there to back him up when he goes to arrest Bradley."

"You think Bradley will go easy?" Clyde asked.

"Would you?" Rusty asked.

"Well, in the first place, I'd never get myself into a predicament like Bradley."

"That ain't the question, Clyde!" Rusty snapped. "What I want to know is...if you was Bradley would you give up peaceable like or would you make a play?"

"I know what the question is," Clyde said with an irritated look. "I was the first one to ask it! Ain't that so, Cole?"

"Matter of fact, I believe you were," Cole said, grinning. "If you want my opinion...I think it all depends on whether or not Bradley thinks we can prove he's guilty. Don't forget he'll still have his chance in a courtroom."

"I almost forgot about that," Rusty admitted. "You think that letter and that piece of paper are enough to convict him?"

"I don't know," Cole said with a slightly concerned look. "It shouldn't be too hard to prove that Bradley wrote the letter, so the best chance for a conviction might boil down to the part where he says he took care of Sally."

"You mean you think he might get away with everything else he's done?" Clyde asked with a stunned look.

"It could happen," Cole said shrugging his shoulders with an uneasy expression.

"Well, that ain't right!"

"What difference does it make, Clyde? As long as he gets convicted of murdering Sally, he'll hang."

"I know that, but it just don't seem right that he might get away with everything else he's done," Clyde said.

"Makes no difference. You can't hang a man twice!" Rusty said with an annoyed look.

\*\*\*

When the stage from Telluride arrived late Thursday afternoon, Cole, Clyde, and Rusty were waiting.

"Good to see you, Amos," Cole said as he shook hands with Amos. "Russell's funeral go alright?"

"Yeah, it was real nice. About half the town showed up to pay their respects," Amos said as he shook hands with Rusty and then Clyde."

"I'm sorry we weren't there," Cole said with an apologetic look. "Anyway, I guess you got my letter."

"Yeah, and you could have knocked me and Jared over with a feather after we read it! I tell you, Cole, these last few days have been sheer hell. First Russell gets killed, then that afternoon I got a telegram from Bradley about Williams and Mike Fish. Tuesday I got your letter and then Wednesday I had to bury one of my best friends."

"You don't really think Bradley shot Williams when he was trying to escape do you?"

"I don't know what to think anymore," Amos said in a slightly flustered tone. "When we got Bradley's telegram, his explanation

116

sounded believable. I felt bad about Mike Fish being killed, but I was glad to hear about Williams getting his. But then after me and Jared read your letter, Bradley's account of what happened started to sound pretty suspicious."

"Any questions about what I wrote in my letter?" Cole asked.

"Not really. You explained things pretty clearly," Amos said. "Have you got that letter and piece of paper with you?"

"No, I had Nicholas lock them up in his safe for safe keeping, but we can go get them if you want to take a look at 'em."

"Not now, but I'll need to take them with me in order to get Judge Tolbert to issue arrest warrants for Putra and Bradley."

"I figured you already had arrest warrants," Cole said with a somewhat surprised look.

"Not yet. We don't need one to make the initial arrests. But we'll have to get a court order to hold them once they're arrested."

"Does that mean you and Jared haven't arrested Joe Putra yet?" Rusty asked.

"Correct. If we did, we couldn't hold him without a court order and we need the evidence you got locked in Grant's safe in order to get one," Amos explained. "But don't you worry...me and Jared will arrest Putra just as soon as I get back to Telluride. Anyway, it's getting late and I'd rather confront Bradley in his office than at his home. I understand he's got a real nice wife. So, maybe we better get on over to the jail and arrest him before he leaves the office," Amos said. "I can look at the evidence after we get him locked up."

"Actually, we've been keeping an eye on him and he already left the office about half an hour ago," Rusty said.

"Well, I guess we can wait until tomorrow morning to arrest Bradley," Amos said. "Might be best to surprise him first thing in the morning after we've all had a good night's sleep, anyway."

"Since we started keeping an eye on him, he's been showing up at the jail right around eight o'clock," Rusty said.

"Okay, what do you say we meet at the café next to the hotel at seven thirty?" Amos suggested. "We'll surprise him as soon as he shows up to open his office."

"We'll be there," Cole said after looking at Rusty and Clyde.

"Make sure you wear those badges Jared gave you," Amos said. "I want Bradley to know he's up against four sworn lawmen and that we mean business as soon as we show up."

# Chapter Twelve

Amos, Clyde, and Rusty were seated at a table by the front window of the café when Cole arrived. Rita walked over to the table as the men exchanged greetings and Cole ordered a cup of coffee.

"I had no idea all of you fellas were lawmen," She said as she noticed that Cole was also wearing a badge. "You men here for some kind of a meeting?"

"Something like that," Amos replied with a blank look.

"I'll be right back with that coffee," Rita said sensing that Amos was not in a talking mood.

Little was said between the men as they drank their coffee and stared out the window waiting for Bradley to show up at the jail. Eight o'clock came and went, but Bradley never showed up.

"What time is it now," Rusty asked after Amos pulled out his pocket watch to check the time for the third time in a span of just a few minutes.

"It's nearly nine o'clock."

"You think he got spooked?" Clyde asked.

"Probably just running late?" Cole said in an optimistic tone.

"He's been pretty punctual the last two days," Rusty added.

"We'll give him another half hour," Amos said as he returned the watch to his pocket.

Time seemed to come to a standstill after that. Rita's periodic trips to the table to refill their coffee cups and Amos's frequent watch checks made each passing minute seem to last forever.

"Nine thirty," Amos finally announced. "I hate to do it, but let's walk over to Bradley's house and see if he's there."

Each of the men left a quarter on the table and thanked Rita as they followed Amos out the door. The sight of four men with badges walking down Main Street caused a lot of curiosity and several of the town's inhabitants stopped to follow the men with their eyes. The Marshal's place was a modest two story house, but the large front porch, picket fence, and new coat of bright yellow paint with white trim made it one of the most attractive houses in town. When the men reached the house, Amos asked Clyde and Rusty to circle around and watch the back. Then after waiting a few minutes, Cole opened the gate and followed Amos to the front door. Both men removed their hats as Amos knocked loudly on the door. Amos was just about to knock again when the door opened and an attractive middle aged woman appeared in the doorway.

"Morning Ma'am, is Marshal Bradley home?" Amos asked.

"No, he's on his way to Telluride," Bradley's wife replied in a pleasant voice.

"Telluride," Amos repeated in a surprised voice. "When did he leave?"

"Early this morning," Mrs. Bradley said with a slightly worried look. "I hope Jonas didn't forget about a meeting or something."

"No Ma'am, I don't think he was expecting us."

"Thank heavens... I'm afraid he hasn't been himself since...Well, I'm sure you know what happened at the jail," Mrs. Bradley said, smiling.

"Yes Ma'am. Was he traveling by stage?"

"No, he left on horseback," Mrs. Bradley said starting to become concerned.

"Did Jonas say when he was coming back?"

"Yes, he said he would be back late on Saturday. What 's this all about?"

"We...uh...we just need to talk to him, Ma'am," Amos said in a stumbling manner.

"What about?"

"We just thought he might have some information about a case we're working on," Amos said in a more confident voice. "Sorry to bother you."

Without any further explanation, Amos promptly turned around to leave and after giving Mrs. Bradley a courteous nod, Cole followed him.

"What the hell would Bradley go to Telluride for?" Amos asked once they were beyond the picket fence.

"I don't know... meet with Putra maybe?" Cole speculated.

"I was afraid you were going to say that," Amos said. "If Jared wasn't busted up, I'd send him a telegram to be on the lookout for Bradley. But, I hate to have him try to take Bradley alone."

"If we hurry we might be able to overtake him," Cole suggested. "I noticed Nicholas keeps a couple of horses in the stable with his mules. I'm sure we could borrow 'em"

"It's worth a try," Amos agreed.

After rounding up Clyde and Rusty, the four men hurried over to Nicholas's warehouse. After a brief conversation with Nicholas, Clyde and Rusty went to the stable to saddle two horses while Amos and Cole followed Nicholas to his office where Nicholas retrieved the letter and piece of paper from his safe. Amos looked over the two documents briefly and then he and Cole rushed over to the stable.

"See you fellas, in a few days," Cole said as he mounted one of the horses.

"Hope you catch the son of a bitch!" Rusty shouted as Cole and Amos started galloping off.

By the time Cole and Amos started after Bradley, he had already been on the road for over two hours. Both Cole and Amos were excellent riders and they kept their horses going at a fast pace, but Bradley was also an accomplished rider and because he was anxious to get to Telluride, he too was pushing his horse hard. As a result, even though Cole and Amos tried their best to overtake Bradley, he reached Telluride a little over thirty minutes ahead of them.

"I want to stop at the jail and fill Jared in," Amos said as they rode into town.

"While you do that, I'll take the horses over to the livery and see that they get rubbed down good, watered, and fed," Cole replied.

"Okay, then why don't you come back to the jail and we'll go arrest Putra. I'd feel better with him in custody."

Cole agreed and when they reached the jail, Amos dismounted and Cole continued to the stable with Amos's horse in tow. Cole returned to the jail a few minutes later and then he and Amos walked the few blocks to a small house where Joe Putra lived alone.

"Doesn't look like he's home," Cole said when they reached the house and saw that it was dark.

"Let's make sure," Amos said.

Cole followed Amos onto the front porch and both men rested their hands on the butts of their pistols as Amos knocked loudly on the door.

"Maybe he went out for dinner," Amos said after knocking several more times and getting no response.

"Why don't we do the same thing and then have a look around town for him," Cole suggested.

Amos agreed and the two of them walked back to Main Street. After having supper at the Smuggler Café, Amos and Cole walked around town looking for Joe Putra and Jonas Bradley. They stopped in at the Yellow Canary and the other saloons, but their search turned up nothing and no one they asked remembered seeing either of the two men. It was after ten o'clock when they walked back to Putra's house and their spirits took a leap when they saw a single light in the front room of the house.

"Joe Putra knows me, so I'll go to the door," Amos said. "Why don't you watch the back just in case he tries to make a run for it?"

Cole agreed and after a short wait to give Cole time to get into position, Amos walked up onto the front porch and knocked on the door.

"Sheriff's department! Open up!" Amos shouted after his knocking received no response.

Amos's repeated knocking and shouting for a few minutes without results and then he walked around to the back of the house.

"You still back here, Cole?" Amos asked loudly.

"Yeah, over here!" Cole replied as he stepped out from behind a row of lilac bushes.

"If he's in there, I can't get him to come to the door."

"I'm sure that lamp wasn't lit the first time we were here," Cole replied. "Maybe, he came and left again. Did you try the door?"

"Yeah, it was locked."

"Should we try the back door?" Cole asked.

"Might as well."

Amos tried the back door and when it opened, both men drew their guns and went inside.

"We know you're in here, Putra!" Amos shouted. "You know me...I'm Deputy Crabtree! Better show yourself before you get hurt!"

After receiving no response, Amos and Cole made their way through the dark kitchen to a hallway where the lamp from the parlor provided some light.

"Looks like there was struggle!" Amos said as he saw the overturned chairs in the front room.

With their backs against the walls and pistols ready, Amos and Cole continued down the hall until they reached the parlor where they saw a broken glass on the floor next to a half full bottle of whiskey laying on its side.

"Better check the bedrooms," Amos whispered as he reached for the kerosene lamb and turned up the wick.

After searching the rest of the house and finding nothing else unusual or out of place, Amos and Cole sat in the parlor waiting for Joe Putra to return. When the clock on the mantle began chimed twelve times they left the house and Cole checked into the hotel while Amos went on home. The next morning Cole met Amos and Jared at the jail and then the three of them walked to Joe Putra's house. When they received no response at the front door, they entered the house through the back door and after discovering the house was exactly as they had found and left it, they walked to Joe Putra's place of business where they were told that Putra hadn't been seen since the close of business on the previous day.

"What now?" Cole asked once they were outside.

"Looks like Putra either skipped or he's the victim of foul play," Amos replied.

"If he skipped, he must have left in a hurry," Amos said.

"Yeah, and he must not have taken anything with him," Jared added. "His closets were still full of clothes."

"I'm bettin' Bradley has something to do with this!" Cole said. "Why else would he have come to Telluride? And where is he?"

"I'm sure you're right," Amos agreed. "Maybe, they both got frogy and skipped out together."

"Yeah or Bradley could be on his way back to Ridgeway," Amos said. "According to his wife, he was gonna be back tomorrow afternoon."

"If he's already on his way back, he'll be back before tomorrow afternoon," Jared said.

"Unless he plans on spending the night in Placerville," Amos said. "What you say we head that way and find out?"

"Might as well," Cole said.

"Wish I could go along," Jared said. "I'd sure like to be there when you slap the cuffs on him. He always was sort of arrogant, like he was better than me just because I was only a deputy."

After saddling their horses, Cole and Amos started for Placerville and arrived shortly after noon. Bill Smith was working the registration desk when Amos and Cole entered the hotel lobby.

"I'm glad to see you Deputy Braxton," Bill Smith said. "Maybe you can tell me what to do with Drew Williams' belongings?"

"As far as I'm concerned, you can give 'em away or throw 'em away," Cole replied.

"You wasn't really a friend of his, was you?"

"Not hardly."

"I kinda figured that out once I found out he was the one that shot Sheriff Douglas."

"Do you know who Marshal Bradley is?" Cole asked.

"Ain't he the one that shot Drew Williams?"

"That's right. Do you know him?"

"No Sir, I seen his name in the paper, but I've never met him... at least not that I remember."

"Then he hasn't checked in here today?" Amos asked.

"No Sir, we ain't had anybody check in under that name."

"What do you want to do, Amos? Stay or go on to Ridgeway?"

"Might as well stay the night," Amos said. "He might show up before the day's over."

"Will one room for the two of you be okay?" Bill Smith asked with an uneasy expression. "I hate to ask, but it is a house rule."

"One room will be fine," Cole said with a slight grin.

122

After receiving their keys, Cole and Amos rode to Mister Luze's barn and arranged to have their horses watered, fed, and stabled for the night. Then they returned to the hotel where they each had a ham sandwich and a beer in the dining hall before settling down on the bench in front of the hotel.

"You think he'll show?" Cole asked after the first hour passed.

"I don't know," Amos replied with a hint of depression in his voice. "If he was in Telluride, seems like we would have run into him. And the fact that we couldn't find Joe Putra either... makes it an even bigger mystery."

"Yeah, I'm guessing the two of them must be somewhere together," Cole said. "You know there's one thing mentioned in that letter which we never really talked about."

"What's that?'

"The letter mentions a hideout...I wonder if Bradley and Putra went to the hideout?"

"Never thought of that, but it makes sense," Amos said in a rejuvenated tone. "They might have had some stolen whiskey stashed at their hideout that they needed to move."

"Yeah and maybe some wagons and mules, too," Cole said.

"If that's the case there's a good chance Bradley will show up here and Putra will show up back in Telluride later today."

"You know Cole, you're pretty good at this. You ever think about becoming a full time lawman?" Amos asked. "Jared is talking about running for sheriff and if he gets elected we'll be looking for another full time deputy."

"No, I'm not interested. Seems to me you fellas got too many rules to follow. I like the old saying... an eye for an eye and a tooth for a tooth. All this business about arrest warrants and court orders seems like a waste of time. I figure if a man commits a murder he deserves to die."

"Well, I wish it was that easy!" Amos chuckled.

Another hour passed and when Amos and Cole spotted a lone rider coming towards the hotel, they both sat up straight.

"Is that him?" Cole asked in an eager voice.

"Can't tell. It sort of looks like him, but I can't be sure. Wish I knew what kind of horse he was on."

"Maybe we better go inside just in case," Cole suggested.

Cole and Amos stood up and made their way back inside as fast as they could without acting suspicious.

"If it is him why don't you duck around the corner and come at him from the front. I'll slip inside the bar room and come up behind him," Cole suggested.

Amos nodded and the two men quickly moved into position. A few minutes later the rider stopped his horse in front of the hotel entrance and after tying it to the hitching rail, he walked into the lobby.

"You need a room?" Bill Smith asked as the man walked up to the registration desk.

"Yeah, I'm the marshal from Ridgeway. Any chance you could give me a private room?"

"Hello Jonas," Amos said as he stepped from around the corner with his gun drawn.

"Amos...what's with the gun?" Bradley asked in a surprised voice as Bill Smith dropped down behind the registration counter.

"Put your hands up, Jonas. You're under arrest."

"Are you crazy? You can't arrest me!" Bradley said as his gun hand started moving toward his gun.

"Better do as he said," Cole said as he stepped into the lobby from the bar room and cocked his pistol.

"What the hell is this all about?" Bradley asked in an angry, but nervous tone after glancing back at Cole.

"I think you know why we're here, Jonas," Amos replied as he took another step toward Bradley.

"I don't know what you're talking about!" Bradley insisted in a loud voice.

"He's talking about murder and whiskey stealing!" Cole said in a tone that said he was growing impatient. "Now quit stalling and put your hands up!"

After hearing the determination in Cole's voice, Bradley glanced over his shoulder one more time and then slowly raised his hands.

"I'll keep him covered, Cole. Go ahead and grab his gun," Amos said.

Cole moved closer and after lifting Bradley's pistol from his holster, Amos holstered his pistol, pulled a pair of handcuffs from his gun belt, and put them on Bradley's wrists.

"You're making a big mistake!" Bradley said in a threatening voice. "I'll have your job for this, Deputy!"

"We'll see about that," Amos replied calmly.

"Don't suppose you would care to tell us where you've been or where Joe Putra is," Cole asked grinning.

"How the hell would I know where Joe Putra is?" Bradley smirked.

124

"Isn't that why you went to Telluride? To meet up with Joe Putra," Cole asked still grinning.

"I don't know what you're talking about!" Bradley said glaring at Cole. "Who the hell do you think you are asking me questions anyway?"

"Cole Braxton is the name."

"He's a sworn deputy, Jonas. He's here to help me take you in," Amos said.

"Yeah well, I'm not answering any of your stupid questions and I want to see a lawyer."

Even though it was late in the afternoon, Cole and Amos decided to take Bradley back to Telluride and lock him up instead of waiting until the following morning. It was late in the evening by the time Bradley was locked up in the county jail, but in spite of the late hour, Amos and Cole walked to Joe Putra's house, anyway. After knocking on the front door and getting no response, they again went through the kitchen door and checked the house, but Putra was not there and everything was still exactly as they had left it.

The following morning, Amos and Jared were both in the sheriff's office when Cole stopped by. The three men exchanged greetings and then they all sat down to drink a cup of coffee.

"I doubt I'll be needing this anymore," Cole said as he laid his badge on the desk. "I'll have Clyde and Rusty drop theirs off next time we bring another load of whiskey to town."

"Me and Jared talked it over and we sure wish you would think about what I said yesterday," Amos said. "If Jared gets elected we'd sure like to have you as a deputy."

"Thanks fellas, I appreciate the offer, but it's like I said, you fellas got way too many rules to worry about."

"Well, the election is still a few months off, so just think about it." Jared said.

"You getting ready to head back to Ridgeway?" Amos asked.

"Yeah, but I'm sure I'll be back in a day or two with a load of whiskey."

"Well, don't be a stranger. Stop by whenever you're in town."

"I imagine I'll be in town pretty regular like from now on," Cole said. "Now that Bradley and his bunch are out of action, Nicholas will likely have us making two runs a week."

"I'll let you know as soon as Bradley's trial date is set," Jared said. "I'm sure you'll be called upon to testify."

"I'm looking forward to it," Cole said smiling.

Once Cole's cup was empty, the three men shook hands and then Cole left.

# Chapter Thirteen

On the day after Jonas Bradley was arrested, Joe Putra's body was found floating in the San Miguel River near Sawpit. Putra had been shot twice with a .44 which coincidentally was the same caliber as Bradley's pistol. With Putra out of business, the job of supplying whiskey to Telluride and the surrounding mining camps fell on Nicholas Grant. As a result, Cole, Clyde, and Rusty started making two trips a week to Telluride in order to keep up with the demand for whiskey. The trips were uneventful and Cole could tell Clyde and Rusty were becoming bored with the routine. So, he was not surprised when the three of them were in the Yellow Canary on the first of September and Rusty broke the news that he and Clyde were going to quit.

"I'm sorry to hear it fellows, but I'm not surprised," Cole said.

"Well, it was a real adventure for a while," Clyde said, grinning, "But drivin' wagons ain't really our line of work. Hell, we're cowboys!"

"I understand," Cole replied smiling.

"And besides that, I figure if we don't get out of here before the snow comes, Clyde is liable to waste all the money he's saved on whiskey and whores," Rusty said with a big grin.

"I reckon one of us has to live up to our reputations as Texas cowboys," Clyde replied with a broad grin.

"When are you planning on leaving?" Cole asked after a short laugh.

"Well, we don't want to leave Nicholas in a bind. He sure helped us out when we was flat broke. So, we figured we'd make one or two more runs to give him time to hire a couple more drivers."

"I know he'll be disappointed when you tell him you're quitting, but he should be able to hire a couple more drivers without any problem, especially now that all the trouble has stopped."

"I heard some of Joe Putra's drivers are still looking for work," Clyde said.

"How about you, Cole? Now that the whiskey war is over, how much longer you reckon you'll keep working for Nicholas?" Rusty asked.

"I don't know. To be honest... since all the trouble has stopped, lately I've been feeling sort of like an extra thumb. Nicholas has been talking about opening another warehouse in Cortez and he'd like me to run it. But I'm kind of like you fellas...running a warehouse it isn't exactly my line of work."

"You could come to Texas with me and Clyde," Rusty said with a hopeful look.

"Hell yeah, we'd be proud to have you as a partner!" Clyde said.

"Be careful...I might just take you up on that offer someday," Cole chuckled.

"You'd be welcome!" Rusty said with a sincere look.

"Well, here's to you fellas. I wish you the best of luck!" Cole said as he lifted his glass.

The three men touched glasses and then downed the contents.

"I've really enjoyed your company," Cole said as he set the glass on the bar.

"We've enjoyed yours too, Cole," Rusty said.

"Yeah, you've been a true friend," Clyde added.

As it turned out, Jonas Bradley's trial started on the very day that Clyde and Rusty left Ridgeway. So, Cole was in Telluride when Clyde and Rusty boarded the train to continue their trip back to Texas. Although the three men had become very close friends and they were sad to part company, saying goodbye was a difficult thing for men of their cut. So, none of them was truly upset about Cole's inability to see Clyde and Rusty off.

During Bradley's trial, it became quite obvious that the county prosecutor was no match for the high priced lawyer from Denver that Bradley hired to defend him. Although in all fairness, with Williams, Putra, and Taylor dead and nothing but circumstantial evidence, the case would have been difficult for even the best of prosecutors. Ultimately, the case revolved around the piece of paper Cole found in Williams' hotel room and the letter. Bradley's attorney had little difficulty discrediting the piece of paper. However, the prosecutor was able to prove that the letter was written by Bradley. But Bradley's attorney successfully lessened the impact when he called Bradley to the witness stand.

"Jonas, you heard Mister Frank, the handwriting expert, testify that in his professional opinion... that letter was written by you." Bradley's attorney said while Jonas Bradley was on the witness stand. "Do you deny that you wrote the letter?"

"No, I'm not going to lie about it," Bradley said in a humble voice. "I wrote the letter."

"Then you admit you were aware that Drew Williams and Bart Taylor robbed those two men from Texas."

"Yes, Williams and Taylor were afraid I would find out that it was them that committed the robbery. So, Williams came to me and offered me some money to let them off the hook."

"Was it a lot of money?"

"It was a hundred dollars," Bradley replied with his head bowed.

"In your fifteen years as an officer of the law, was that the first time you ever took money for...looking the other way?"

"Yes, it was the first and only time," Bradley replied in a remorseful tone. "And taking that money was the stupidest thing I've ever done. I only wish those two Texans were here today, so I could apologize to them."

"Now in that letter you mentioned a woman named Sally...who was Sally?"

"Her name was Sally Larson," Bradley replied.

"What was Sally Larson's profession?"

"She worked in the Galloping Goose Saloon."

"In other words, she was a prostitute!" Bradley's attorney said in a dramatic voice.

"Yes, that's right."

"Your Honor, would you have the court clerk read part of the letter?" Bradley's attorney asked the judge. "I'd like to hear the part where it starts out...they don't know I'm involved..."

The judge nodded and the clerk started to read the designated portion of the letter aloud.

"They don't know I'm involved," the clerk read aloud. "So, I'll take care of Sally to make sure it stays that way."

"Thank you, Sir," Bradley's attorney said to the clerk. Then turning to Bradley he asked, "What exactly did you mean by that, Jonas?"

"Sally was the one that put Williams and Taylor up to robbing those two Texans and when she found out that Williams paid me to look the other way, she tried to blackmail me."

"So, you killed her!" Bradley's attorney exclaimed.

"No, of course not!" Bradley insisted with a mortified expression. "All she wanted was a hundred dollars. So, I just gave her the money Williams gave me. I felt bad about taking it, anyway. So, I didn't really mind losing it."

"Now remember, Jonas...you're under oath," Bradley's attorney said. Then after a theatrical pause, he asked, "Did you kill Sally Larson?"

"Absolutely not! I admit I made a mistake by taking that money in the first place. But, what kind of a man would kill a woman over a hundred dollars?"

"Now Jonas, according to the report that you yourself wrote on Sally Larson's murder...Sally Larson was stabbed multiple times."

"That's right.

"Was the murder weapon ever found?"

"No, I figured the murderer took it with him when he fled."

"I've noticed that it's quite common for men to carry knives along with their pistols on their gun belts. Did you ever carry a knife on your gun belt?

"No, I never had any reason to," Bradley replied.

Bradley's trial ended a few hours later and it took the jury less than an hour to deliver a verdict. Bradley was found guilty of accepting a bribe for which the judge sentenced Bradley to one year in the Colorado Penitentiary and all the other charges were dismissed.

Cole was so disgusted that he could barely speak and the disappointment on Amos and Jared's face was obvious as they led Bradley out of the courtroom. They met later at the Yellow Canary to commiserate over a few drinks, but the whiskey did little to comfort them.

"We all know that son of a bitch is guilty!" Cole said.

"Yeah and I think the judge and at least half the other people in the courtroom would agree with you...including the jury," Jared said. "But, even you admitted it was a weak case. All the evidence except the letter was circumstantial."

"I know, but that doesn't change the fact that Bradley got away with murdering four men and a woman!"

"Well Cole, don't get me wrong, I'd like to see Bradley hang for killing Sally Larson, Mike Fish, and Dan Brewer, but he probably did us a favor by killing Williams and Putra. Otherwise those bastards would probably have gotten off with just a slap on the hand, too."

"Yeah, but if they were still alive maybe one of them would have rolled over on Bradley!"

"I guess we'll never know," Amos said.

"You give my offer any more thought?" Jared asked trying to change the subject. "I'm pretty sure I've got the sheriff's job in the bag and I'd sure like to have you as a deputy."

"Being a lawman isn't for me. Too many rules," Cole replied. "I probably should have shot that bastard, Bradley, when I had the chance!"

"Well, I admit not everybody gets the justice they deserve, but the odds are still on our side." Jared said.

"Yeah, maybe so, but I just have a hard time doing nothing when we all know Bradley is guilty of murder."

"Well, you best just let it go, Cole. We gave it our best shot and there's nothing else we can do about it now." Jared said. "How about another shot of whiskey?"

"No, I best be heading back to Ridgeway," Cole said in a dejected tone. "Nicholas is anxious for me to make a whiskey run with those two new drivers he hired."

In the weeks that followed the trial, the town of Ridgeway hired a replacement marshal for Jonas Bradley and Nicholas hired four additional new drivers to keep up with the growing demand for whiskey. The whiskey shipments to Telluride continued to be uneventful, which Nicholas was convinced was in part due to Cole's reputation. So, Cole continued to accompany all of the shipments to Telluride.

In late September the first snowfall blanketed the region making the road from Placerville to Telluride impassible for a few days. Shipments continued after that, but the unpredictable weather and subsequent storms made regular shipments impossible.

Weeks later, Jared and Amos were in the office huddled around the potbellied stove drinking coffee. They both turned toward the door as it opened letting in a blast of cold air.

"Well hello, Cole!" Jared said as Cole stepped inside and quickly closed the door behind him.

"How are you fellas?" Cole replied as he joined them by the stove.

"Help yourself to a cup of coffee," Amos said as he pointed to the spare cups hanging from pegs on the wall.

"Thanks, I think I'll take you up on it," Cole said as he reached for a cup. "Feels like we got another storm blowing in."

"Yeah, probably get some more snow before morning," Amos replied.

"By God, this coffee will sure put hair on your chest!" Cole said after taking a gulp of coffee. "This stuff is as thick as axle grease."

"Amos always makes it that stout," Jared chuckled.

"I heard you made it in with another whiskey shipment last night," Jared said grinning. "What's it been a week?"

"Yeah, about that. This weather sure has made it tough to keep drivers," Cole said cupping his hands around the hot cup. "Anyway, it was my last trip, too."

"What do mean, this is your last trip?" Jared asked in a surprised voice.

"I'm calling it quits," Cole said with a big smile. "Time to move on."

"I thought you were going to take Nicholas up on his offer to open that warehouse in Cortez!" Amos said.

"Well, Nicholas and my sister almost had me talked into it. But I just couldn't convince myself to take a job where I'd be inside all day."

"I'd sure rather be inside on a day like this than sitting' on a wagon seat," Jared chuckled.

"Yeah well, won't be long before the railroad reaches Telluride and once it does, there won't be any more whiskey hauling jobs, anyway. Men like me will be extinct!" Cole laughed.

"That reminds me of that corny joke, Clyde used to tell," Amos laughed. "He ever tell you that joke, Jared?"

"The one about the mama skunk and the two baby skunks?" Jared asked, laughing. "Yeah, unfortunately I heard it several times. It wasn't even funny!"

"The only thing funny about it was hearing Clyde tell it," Amos said still laughing. "I sure miss Clyde and Rusty."

"They were a couple of real characters, alright," Jared agreed.

"You ever hear from those two since they left, Cole? " Amos asked.

"Yeah, I got a letter from Rusty about a week ago," Cole said after taking his last swig of coffee. "Sounds like they got themselves a nice ranch going down on the Pecos River. Matter of fact, that's where I'm headed."

"Well, I'll be damned!" Amos said with a trace of envy in his eyes. "So, you're gonna be a cow puncher again."

"Yeah and I guess they got a problem with cattle rustlers down there," Cole said smiling again. "So, I thought I'd see if I couldn't help Clyde and Rusty put an end to the problem."

"You aren't planning to ride a horse all the way down there are you?" Jared asked when he noticed Cole's horse tied out front.

"No, but I been riding on a wagon seat for so long, I figured I best get used to being in the saddle again. So, I thought I'd travel by horseback until my backside has had enough and then I'll catch a train the rest of the way. Anyhow, I guess I better be on my way. I want to get over the pass before the snow starts falling."

"Well, I hate to see you go, Cole," Amos said extending his hand. "Give Clyde and Rusty our best and drop us a line when you get settled."

"I'll do that," Cole said as he shook hands with Amos.

"Good luck to you, Cole," Jared said as he and Cole shook hands.

"Thanks, Jared and good luck to you in the election, too," Cole said grinning. "I know you'll make a good sheriff."

Cole walked to the door and then paused as if there was more to be said. Then he smiled and gave a casual wave as he opened the door.

Three weeks later, Jared was elected as the new county sheriff. On the day after the election, Jared was in his office with a reporter from the San Miguel Examiner who was just finishing his interview.

"I guess that about does it, Sheriff. I appreciate you taking time to answer my questions," the reporter said as he was putting on his heavy coat.

"Happy to do it, Bob," Jared replied as he shook hands with the reporter.

"By the way, did you hear about Jonas Bradley?" the reporter asked in a casual voice.

"Yeah, I got a letter from the prison warden advising me that Bradley was being paroled next month," Jared said with a disgusted expression.

"No, I mean did you hear somebody killed him?"

"Bradley's dead?" Jared asked with a surprised look. "What happened?"

"There was an article about it in the Canon City Gazette," the reporter replied. "We decided to reprint it in today's paper. Since Bradley was from Ridgeway, we thought it might be of interest to some of our readers. I got a copy with me if you want to read it for yourself."

"Thanks," Jared said with a stunned expression.

"Well thanks again, Sherriff," the reporter said as he handed Jared a copy of the paper and left.

Once the reporter was gone Jared went to his desk and opened the paper. He scanned the first page and turned to the second.

"Prison Inmate Killed by Unknown Assassin," Jared read aloud. "On November fourteen, an inmate at the Colorado State Prison Farm, west of Cannon City, was killed by an unknown assassin. Prison inmate, Jonas Bradley, who was serving a one year sentence for accepting a bribe while serving as the town marshal of Ridgeway, was shot to death early in the morning while feeding livestock. Bradley was recently moved from the state penitentiary in Cannon City to the prison farm due to his prior law enforcement status and was scheduled for early release in December. Officials initially suspected that Bradley was killed by another prisoner. However, an autopsy revealed that Bradley was killed by a large caliber rifle bullet, leading prison officials to believe that Bradley had been shot by an outsider and the case was turned over to the Fremont County Sheriff. After hearing of the incident, well-known local rancher, Don Harper reported finding fresh tracks and a single 45-75 cartridge on a high butte west of the prison farm. Sheriff Hank Weston visited the sight of the discovery, but determined that the tracks were probably made by a deer hunter and unrelated to the case, since no ordinary man could make

133

a shot from such a distance. According to Sheriff Weston, the shooting remains a mystery with no leads or suspects."

A broad smile crept across Jared's face as he finished reading the article and set the paper aside.

"Cole Braxton was certainly no ordinary man!" Jared chuckled.

**The End**

**A note from the author, Norm Bass:**

Thank you for reading *The Whiskey Haulers.* I hope you enjoyed the story and as always, thanks for keeping the spirit of the old west alive. You can e-mail me at hookedb@hotmail.com or follow me on Twitter.


**Other books by Norm Bass:**

Justice Rides A Spotted Horse
Beneath The Rustler's Moon (Vol. I - The Gentry Brothers Series)
Tin Cup Justice (Vol. II - The Gentry Brothers Series)
They Hung An Innocent Man (Vol. III - The Gentry Brothers Series)
Cactus Casanovas
South Of The Pecos
Beyond The Pecos
The Bounty Hunters From Coffin Creek
Last Stage To Cactus Flats

Made in the USA
San Bernardino, CA
21 December 2015